My Life
on the Fringe:

a journey into design

My Life on the Fringe:

a journey into design

Randy Trull (signature)

Randy Trull

edited by
Robert Hill Camp & Susan Taylor Block

for my mother,
Mabel Holland Trull

Contents

Preface

"THE ROAD LESS TRAVELED" is one most of us only dream about. Robert Frost coined that phrase, and my friend lives it. His friends call him Randy, but his given name is Randolph Holland Trull...and don't forget it. When I think of Randy, I think about what the lead character said in that great play, *Mame*: "Life is a banquet and most poor suckers are starving to death."

Randy partook of the feast immediately and proved himself to be one of America's finest fabric designers, before turning his attention to apparel and house furnishings. The existence and versatility of his creative genius cannot be denied. He likes to refer to himself as "crazy," but I am here to tell you: Randy Trull is about as crazy as the proverbial fox.

When Randy asked me to write the preface for *My Life on the Fringe*, I was honored, but when I sat down at my desk to write it, I broke out into a cold sweat. His life is so full of experiences and his personality is truly beyond description. How could I sum him up in just a few pages? I decided just to spit it all out.

Randy Trull

I have known Randy Trull for over thirty years. Unlike so many other friendships that blur with time, my relationship with Randy continues to endure. Truly, he has never met a stranger, and he, himself, is that "one of a kind" person you want to meet again and again. He is disarming, opinionated, arrogant, stylish, colorful—and totally unforgettable.

This book is aptly named. Randy has lived a life of contradictions and moves easily in and out of two worlds. His flamboyant style has put off some of the uptight suit-and-tie corporate types, but his confidence of purpose has often redeemed him. Some of his competitors learned the hard way that what they interpreted as a head full of naiveté actually was a driven, calculating mind. With the power of his unusual personality alone, he managed to turn many of his skeptics into some of his best golfing buddies.

I am reminded of a time when most of the industry executives were invited to a major charity event. An important California retailer sponsored the benefit at a prestigious golf club. On the opening day, guests were mulling around, reviewing the lists of foursomes, when in strolls R. Holland Trull. He arrived the only way he knew how: to great attention. He was dressed almost wholly in pink! His slacks, shirt, sweater, socks, golf bag, and club covers were all pink. His shoes were off-white, but that only seemed to accentuate all that pink. He got what he wanted, and did it with style. Everyone noticed him—he wore the odd ensemble beautifully—and, I'd guess no one ever forgot him.

Randy has a knack for fitting into any situation. He was at home in board rooms making detailed presentations, and he was just as comfortable walking the factory floor. He hobnobbed with European royals and the American elite, yet he was kind and generous to many ordinary folks who happened to cross his path.

I met Randy just after he was named design director for Croscill, in the 1970s. At that time, Croscill could be categorized as an up-and-coming textile company on the cusp of breaking out. All they needed was a good hard kick in the butt, and Randy Trull provided that kick. He transformed the company. Here he was, a Southern Protestant working for a New York Jewish family business. He certainly stirred up the "knish pot."

Working tirelessly at Croscill, Randy created everything from a "new look" showroom to color-coordinated lines. He travelled all over the country telling the company's story, conducting seminars, presenting critiques—and, always, selling. His dedication, professionalism, and strong work ethic, in conjunction with his unorthodox personality helped put Croscill on the map.

Randy's always had the good sense to balance work and play. While at Croscill, he purchased a wonderful old yacht and found time to refit and decorate it. He sailed up and down the Eastern Seaboard. He vacationed in Monaco with his dear friend Rosita and stopped in London to spend some time at his flat, take in some West End shows, and shop the antique stores.

As his professional status and economic comfort level grew, Randy's ambition remained keen. He was gratified that his creative talents were recognized, but not content to rest on last year's line or his current list of decorating clients. His creative ideas continued to flow and his client list grew to include more and more famous people, many of whom came to call him their friend. Catherine Von Bomel

Randy Trull

of the Breyer's Ice Cream family invited Randy to attend a black tie affair at the Waldorf Astoria. When he arrived, his hostess sat him between Jackie Kennedy and Senator John F. Kennedy. That is indicative of the respect he gained throughout his career.

Let us not forget that Randolph Holland Trull is, above all else, a true Southern boy. He grew up in Raleigh, North Carolina during the 1930s and early 1940s. I do believe those years set the foundation for his success and prepared him for the full and exciting career he has enjoyed. Good breeding played its part. Conservative attitudes, home training in what was good and proper, and easy-going country club life were the norm in Randy's world. No matter how comfortable that felt, Randy knew from an early age that he would have to leave Raleigh in order to follow his dream. His mother's support, love, and encouragement went far to help him achieve his goals.

So, off went young Randy to New York City. He enrolled in Parsons School of Design to learn the techniques he would need for his career path. U.S. Navy duty interrupted his schooling for a year and a half, then he returned to Parsons and graduated in 1954. That over, he set out to capture New York. Randy doesn't talk about emotions much, but New York holds a special place in his heart.

No matter how busy with work or play he was, Randy always found time for his parents. He was a loving son to both of them, but he was exceptionally close to his mother, who was his most ardent admirer. She visited him often in New York and he accompanied her to Europe several times. His mother's unsuccessful battle with cancer pained Randy terribly and incited the only tears I ever saw him shed.

As his father aged, Randy made sure he had the best care

and lots of respect. In time, Randy became the patriarch of the family—the "go-to guy." On occasion, he mediated squabbles, but, he always was, and is, there for them. Randy has always said that family is very important to him, and his is no exception. Sometimes family politics don't go his way, but he has a hard time holding a grudge.

He's heading towards eighty now, and as vibrant and enthusiastic as ever. Occasionally, he flies to New York and we meet for lunch. He recently recounted his latest travels to me. He flew to Sweden to visit the Ludvigsons, proceeded to purchase a Volvo, then drove all over Europe. He visited Rosita in Monaco and friends in Italy, then bought antiques and caught some shows in London. The antiques were shipped to Wilmington, NC, where Randy currently lives, and many of them have already sold at his popular antiques and accessories store, Classic Designs of Wilmington. As usual, he caters to the elite—and, oh, did I tell you? If you want to work with Mr. Trull himself, it is by appointment only!

What more can I say that Aunt Mame hasn't already?

—Chip Scala

And Now a Word from Randy

WELL, NOW I HAVE STEPPED OUT of the box for sure! Writing a book about my life has been a very different sort of challenge. I thought it best to keep most of my fantasies to myself, but I have shared many wild things that did actually happen to me. For almost eighty years, I have lived a life that is different. I have not lived in the center of conformity or at the outer edges of extremism. I have simply lived...on the fringe.

When I was a child, my father once told me that he would rather be a big shot in a small town than be a little shot in a big town, but that was just not the way I was going to let it happen. Though I loved my family and enjoyed living in Raleigh, NC, I kept dreaming of a bigger world where I would fashion my way to success. As soon as I was old enough, I followed those dreams. Eventually, I became somewhat of a big shot in a very big town.

I hope reading *My Life on the Fringe* will inspire others to step out of the box and live life reaching for what we think we were born to achieve. We only travel down this road once and I think it is best to live a lot.

1 | *Modest Beginnings and Good Role Models*

THEY SAY MOST PEOPLE have a lucky number. If that is true, then mine must be seven, since I was born in the seventh month, on the seventh day, in the seventh hour, and even in the seventh minute. Though I have lied about my age for years, I am now seventy-nine, and was born in 1930. You should know how it pains me to tell the truth when it comes to my age, as I am now an old man. I still try to pretend that I am just a kid, but what a joke that is.

I was born to parents who were trying to carve out a place in their community, for themselves, and for their two children. When you realize that I was born in 1930, and it was the height of the Great Depression, I am quite sure that my parents were really having a tough time for those first couple of years. My father seemed to have found his place in business early on, for whatever reason, when he went into the plumbing and heating business with his older brother, my uncle Roy. My mother was, to say the very least, a very active woman who was involved in many different things.

When it comes to recounting history, I guess that we

Monk Trull, an easy-going man with a dry sense of humor, is pictured here in Raleigh, about 1924.

This photo of Mabel Trull was taken in 1924, when she was a student at Buies Creek Academy, now Campbell University. The school's founder, Archibald Campbell, was a Holland relative.

would all like to go back and change some things in our past, but these are a part of our own personal history, like them or not. One thing I would not want to change were my parents, who really did a great job with us. When you are older, you look back and think what great parents you had, but I didn't come to that decision recently. Even as a child, I always thought that my mother and father were the best. I just wish that I had expressed my love and respect for them more early on.

My family would have been considered poor in those days. They lived in a house and drove a car, but they really couldn't afford either. I have heard it said many times that my Aunt Pauline used to come over with food, set it on the kitchen table, and then go visit in the living room. Since Aunt Pauline was my father's older sister, and her husband, Clifton, was making enough money working for the railroad, they helped ensure that we had enough food on the table. At the time, I had no idea, since I was only a child, and the youngest at that.

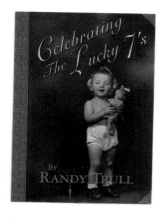

When I was born, they had just built a brand new brick house in what was considered the "right" neighborhood in Raleigh — Hayes Barton. I think that my parents rented out half of the house for a short time, though I can't verify that. If my memory serves me well, or if you can believe childhood memories, it is true.

Randy Trull chose this photo of himself as the cover for his 70th birthday party program. Even as a toddler, he showed promise for being a very interesting and rather unconventional man.

In 1930, my mother somehow bought a silver and china shop that had gone into bankruptcy, on Main Street in Raleigh. She had to give the bank a deposit before she took

Home sweet Arilginton Street home!

possession, and had ninety days to pay the remaining balance the creditors demanded. She was not only able to do this, she was also able to make enough of a profit on this venture that she paid the debt off early. She also paid back a loan to Uncle Clifton, and even had enough left to make several overdue mortgage payments on the house. She really knew the value of that inventory, and could make a deal. She had foresight, too.

Things got better for us when the Depression began to slide away. Business picked up for Dad and my uncle, and Mother began work as a state government employee. As always, she was looking for us to be at the top of things. She came up with the idea of joining the Carolina Country Club. It was brand new and Mother and Dad became charter members. I was just a kid then, but I knew it gave me one more place to go and see what mischief I could devise.

Monk Trull's business fueled the family's transition to more comfortable living.

Mabel and her two sons, Jimmy and Randy, stand in front of their Arlington Street residence about 1937. Mabel designed the appliqué dress.

The country club was the perfect place for Mother. She was wise and had style. Believe me, I could not hold a candle to her example. She would let gentlemen hold the door for her, or light her cigarette (something she should have given up), and was fiercely independent, but she always expected to be treated as a lady should be. Although she has been dead for many years, mother Mabel will be a part of my life forever. I will never forget this was a first-class lady.

A change of seasons always involved some changes around our house. When May came around, all the furniture would be clad in slip covers, the summer curtains would go up, but at the end of the month, we were packed up and sent to the mountains for the summer, as school was out. I always wondered why she did all that work in the house when we would close it up, come back in September, and change it all back again.

I had a "big brother," James Everett Trull, whom we called "Jimmy" until he was much older. (To tell the truth, I don't think I ever called him "Jim.") Jimmy was a great guy and a chip off the old block. When I look back at some of the pictures of father and my brother when they were younger, it is easy to see just how much they looked alike. They even parted their hair in the middle the same way, and were about both about 5'11" tall. They were good looking men, with nice smiles and complexions. I didn't have

It's hard to find any of Randy in Monk Trull's face, but his son, Jimmy, bore a strong resemblance.

the real man's look, since I was so light, with blonde, curly hair and blue eyes. Jimmy even followed my father into his chosen profession in the heating business, where he stayed until his surprising death in 1968, at only thirty-nine. He left a wife and two children.

As the second child, I was known as "the baby." To this day, they refer to my brother as Jimmy, and to me as Ran, the baby. Growing up with an older brother can really be hard, but I was one of the lucky ones. Jimmy was always considerate of me, and truly loving as he watched over me. He rarely even said, "No."

I never felt that I was close to my father. Our natures were very different. We did not even worry about the same things. In fact, he called me "worry wart," because things that bothered or annoyed me went right over his head. He was still a great father, but it was my brother who was so much like him. I was so much like Mother that it was almost like two versus two if there were disagreements. My father always thought I would never learn how to make a living, but he was wrong. He did know I could spend money and live it up, though. Some things haven't changed that much, but I realized my creative side was the path for me to make a good living and enjoy myself doing it.

My name is Randolph, but when I was younger, they would always say, "Hey, Ran,"—never Randolph—and that stuck with me until I went off to school in New York. There, they called me Randy, not Randolph, and it suited me much better. Strange, but you never seem to grow up in your relative's eyes. They think of you one way, and it is in their heads forever.

Shared interests and natures created a natural pull in the Trull house between Monk and Jimmy, and Mabel and Randy.

Mabel Trull's close friend, Jo Stevens Nash (Mrs. Roland Nash), sits here in the Trull's living room, as she often did.

Both my parents were involved in the community, and in whatever things that both my brother and I were doing. We ate dinner together as a family every evening. Even though I had a buddy right down the street, if I wanted to eat dinner at his house, I had to ask mother if it was all right. She would speak to his mother just to make sure there was a real invitation, and that we were both not just making something up. Mother was always careful to check on my friends and see that they were "the right type of people" for me to hang around. She was very clever about how she managed me when it came to behavior, too.

This came about when I began to let on that there was a neighbor's daughter I kind of liked. I later came to realize that Mother did not approve of her, or her family. Instead of saying this outright, Mother just made sure that I had something to do, somewhere to be, or provided a distraction nearly every time there was a chance I'd have idle time to go visit her. I think that the girl's father was a drunk, so Mother knew there could be trouble. She didn't want me involved with the family, if only because I might take the wrong path, or because possible gossip could result from my involvement with the girl.

When you are only a child and you are growing up in a small town in the South, the rest of the world does not exist. You are just living in your little world and thinking about your day, how you are going to spend it in Raleigh, North Carolina. On Saturdays, Mother would give me a quarter to go to the movies. It took a nickel to ride the bus downtown, a dime for the movie, another nickel for candy, and another for the bus ride home. By the time I got home, I'd had a full day—and it only cost Dad twenty-five cents.

Meanwhile, my parents had enjoyed a full day on the

Above: Onslow Club, Labor Day, 1937, (Mabel third from left). This photo was taken at a Shriners' Retreat, possibly at Snead's Ferry, NC. Monk Trull served a term as president of the Wake County Shrine Club.

Jimmy and Randy Trull (left to right) are joined by friend Ann McKenzie in Atlantic Beach, about 1935. Ann later married Jimmy.

Looking svelte and stylish, Mabel Holland Trull stands on the strand at Atlantic Beach, about 1935.

golf course, so everyone was happy. We settled in for the evening, and no one even locked the front door. We never thought about some unwelcome person walking into our house, and, besides, we knew everyone who lived anywhere near us. A stranger would really have stuck out.

Mother and Father told me what to do, and worked at this together. Mother was the disciplinarian, but both were very involved with every aspect of my life. Dad was just another one of the guys in a small town who did what they all did back at that time: He joined all the local clubs, was a Mason, a Shriner, and went to lunch on Monday at the Lions Club. He played golf with his buddies on the weekends, and he just sort of handled me and my brother the way my mother, the boss, told him to.

Years later, I was talking with some friends of my father's and one cleared up something for me. Laughing, this fellow said that Daddy never had the privilege of telling his children that they could do anything. Evidently, Mother would tell them "Yes," but if she didn't want them to do whatever it was they had asked permission for, she would tell them to go ask their father. Then she would tell dad to say "No," so we thought Dad was really mean, as he never said yes to anything we asked him.

Mother worked when we were younger, but she also felt the need to set a good example for us in civic and Christian service. I remember that she was always in the middle of something—local politics, running a business, church functions—but she never failed to put family first. She was beautiful, smart, hard-working, and had a great talent for making things happen when she needed them to. She was a woman who genuinely wanted a career and a family, and I think, at times, she had a very difficult time trying to figure out how to blend the two roles. Mabel Holland Trull was also something special to look at: hazel eyes, brown hair, and a great figure and smile that made the men want to know her well.

She was elected to the Wake County Board of Elections, and was the first woman to serve in such a role in the state of North Carolina. She also served as secretary to the board for fifteen years. She did not need "women's liberation" to pave the way for her, as she did anything she felt like doing, and made her own way through sheer will and effort. I think that she thought politics was exciting, and she was involved with it most of her life. This was a time when most women did not speak out or get involved, but Mother Mabel was not one of those. She told them just what she thought, and backed it up with action.

Once, there was going to be a vote about appointing a black registrar. There were only three people on the board, and the other two had each spoken out that they did not agree with electing a black woman to the position. Because of this, mother's vote was going to make the difference, as it needed to be unanimous. As she sat at home the night before the vote, she said that all people are equal, whether black or white, and that she would vote on behalf of this registrar. Right was right, in her eyes, and wrong was wrong.

When it came right down to it, I always identified more with my mother than my father. Dad's business was undoubtedly an important thing, and a large part of our income, but the heating business never really interested me. Mother's antiques shop was fascinating to me, however, and may have been the basis for my interest in design. The furnishings and variety of items in the shop gave me a never-ending supply of design elements, from which I created patterns in my mind. I was able to imagine the way in which these blended, and could be changed to fit different scenarios, and this began to foster my creativity. I am sure that this, ultimately, lead to my profession and success. I wish that I could have been more like my mother, but to tell the truth, most people felt we were very much alike.

Mother's father was a tough old guy, and the only one he would listen to was my mom. Now this may be hard to believe, as she was his daughter, but he listened to her, and she was firm when she spoke to him. This was mostly about things that needed fixing, maintaining, or replacing, but whatever needed doing, she told him about it. Once she even threatened to take grandmother and move out unless he repainted the walls in several rooms of the house immediately. They had fights, but most of the time, mother would win as he knew she was right.

Although I was afraid of my grandfather when I was younger, as I grew older, he and I became close. When I was in my early twenties (about 1956), and had become pretty successful in the New York design world, we began an interesting tradition. When I would call and plan a trip home from New York, my grandparents would expect not only a visit, but for me to come by and take them to lunch. My mother would let them know I was going to come home, and then later call me to let me know that they were already sitting out on their front porch in the rocking chairs, all dressed and ready to go to out with me. It became a regular thing, and really special.

Granddaddy and I talked about stock investments—he loved southern train stocks, like Seaboard Air Line Railroad. Once when we were talking, he said that he had not received his dividend check. He said that he had read about a fire in the Richmond, Virginia train yard, and that he was sure that his check had burned up with the cars damaged. Since I was also an investor in the same company, and had received my check, I knew that probably wasn't true, but I couldn't resist teasing him about the fact that he'd lost his.

Grandfather was not terribly well—or so people thought, since he retired so early. He stopped building houses in 1928, when he was not even fifty, but did not die until 1976. He could not have been really sick, in his mind or body, since he was able to build a recreational vehicle (trailer) on his own, and he towed that thing all over the country on vacations. When I asked the doctor what had gotten to him when he finally died, and the physician just said, "Old age." He was ninety-six at the time, and his death bed was only the third time he had ever been in the hospital. I hope I have some of those genes.

He loved his cars, but really kept them for a long time. Once, I asked him why he didn't replace the old one he'd had for years. He replied, "Because there ain't nothing wrong with that one." He stayed so active that he was totally un-aware of his age, too. Once, I went by his house for a visit, and saw that he had a huge new dent in his car fender. I asked him what had happened, and he commented that "Some stu-pid old battle axe hit me." I asked him how old she was, and he said, "ninety-two." I couldn't resist chuckling, consider-ing the fact that he was about eighty-eight, himself, at the time. He and grandmother were the oldest living couple in Raleigh until 1976, when they died. They passed on only six weeks apart, and were married for seventy-one years.

Now that I think about them, a funny story comes to mind. When Granddad was eighty-nine, the hospital called my mother in the middle of the night to tell her that some-thing had happened to him. Mother immediately rushed to

Mr. and Mrs. J. E. Holland, Randy's maternal grandparents, are pictured here after one of their many anniversary parties.

the hospital and found that he had ruptured a blood vessel in his neck. She asked my grandmother what he'd been doing that caused him to break a blood vessel in his throat at that time of night. Grandmother answered, "Having sex," to which Mother said, "For heaven's sake, do it in the afternoon, then you won't have to get us all up in the middle of the night!" Grandmother simply replied, "Your father likes to do it after dark." What a guy!

Events and relatives are pretty common ways to remember and frame childhood memories, but I was also very self-aware in that I knew I was somehow different. From the time I was a little boy, I liked to look like I came out of a fashion magazine, and my mother was always very intent on her children being dressed to a "T." Each week, we had very set plan: Go to Sunday school, then head to the country club for lunch.

Every now and then, when I look back on it, I think my

Below Left: "I have no idea why I was wearing a majorette costume," said Randy.

Above: Dressed for dinner at the country club, Jimmy, Mabel, and Randy Trull exude 1930s style.

The Carolina Country Club building the Trulls frequented burned a few years after this photo was taken. The clubhouse that replaced it still stands today.

mother wanted her two children to look as good as any of the other children at the club. Sunday was "dress-up" day, and we did just that even if we wanted to simply play with toys. Jimmy was anything but a dress-up kid. In fact, he was like Alfalfa—a country kid with a wonderful smile and a happy face, who preferred comfortable, basic clothes to "dressy" ones.

When I was a little boy, I kept Mother and Dad on their toes, and, sometimes, drove them a little mad. One Sunday evening, when we were eating at home, I sat there in my seat at the dining room table and told Mother that I did not like what she had fixed. (I think the problem that night was that she'd burned the food.) She just looked at me and said, "Eat your dinner. Do you realize that there are thousands of children starving to death in China who would love to have a meal like this?"

"Name one!" I answered.

Randy's great-aunt Betty Holloman, Mrs. Stevens, (unknown), and his grandmother Lilly Brown Holland create a charming southern portrait. Taken by Monk Trull.

Dad laughed, but then composed himself. "Don't talk to your mother that way," was what he spoke, but the look on his face said, "What am I going to do with this kid?"

At one point, Jimmy got a bicycle for Christmas, and I got a sidewalk bike (a small-framed and small-wheeled bike designed for flat surfaces—no longer made today). Both were good presents, except that I could not ride the damn sidewalk bike and keep up with him, since it had such small wheels. Slowly, I learned how to ride, and then luck came my way. I parked it across the street from where we lived, where they were building a new house. I leaned it against a brick pile, and thank you Lord, a truck driver drove right over it and mashed it flat. What a lucky break for me—even though I threw a fit, I was really glad to be rid of it. My father decided that he'd had enough of this mess, so he gave me Jim's bike, and got him one with even bigger wheels. It didn't really matter that they were bigger—I could now keep up with him. So this spoiled little brat got his way. See, I said I was lucky!

As a family, we always did things together, and my parents took us all

In 1937, Randy "designed" a way to get a bigger bicycle—but his mother was still fashioning his upscale wardrobe.

over the place to show us the world as they knew it. Dad bought a great big Packard, and we had great fun in it. We played all kinds of games in the back seat, and it was almost like a playpen for us when we would travel. I remember that just before we left on one car trip to Atlantic City, New Jersey, Jimmy was out in the yard and stepped on some boards that had nails sticking out. Since he managed to step on two boards, and stuck a nail in both feet, Dad had to carry him most of the trip.

My mother loved those auctions they had along the boardwalk. She would go out for hours and leave Jimmy and me alone with our father. During one of those times, I got a little bored and I proceeded to walk into the auction house. She was sitting up front, right by the auctioneer, and I paraded right by her and up onto the auction platform. I proceeded to lecture her that this was our vacation and that we weren't having a very good time. She tried to pull me down off the platform, but I told her that we were to going to leave her there and have our own vacation. What could you say to a precocious, blonde, little four-year-old boy giving you a lecture? The auctioneer loved it, and everybody there laughed, except for my mother, who looked like she could have strangled me! My father probably stood in the back and laughed, too. He may have put me up to it, but I don't remember for sure.

Once, something went wrong with the Packard. Dad took it down to the repair shop and had it fixed, then brought it home. After the repair, Mother drove it for only another week, then had to call Dad to tell him that it was sitting out on Saint Mary's Street, dead. In utter disgust, he went down and bought a new Dodge for Mother. The Packard was taken to the garage, and they worked on it for a whole week. The mechanics eventually called Dad to tell him that the only thing wrong with the car was that it was out of gas. It was not one of the happier days in our family's history.

2 | *Life in the Thirties*

WHEN I GOT A BIT OLDER, I joined the Boy Scouts, but I am not quite sure why. I was not particularly interested in camping, or learning any outdoor skills, but I was always willing to try new things. They had something interesting called a "Jamboree," where we were to camp out for the weekend, so I signed up for this event. When I arrived at the gate of the campground, the men told me to take all my gear out of the car and put it on my back. I asked if they were mad, as I had mother's car filled to the roof with what I thought I would need for the weekend (today I still pack too much stuff to go places). Well, they said I got no points towards my next badge because I could not carry all my stuff on my back. I told them, "Who cares. I need it all for the weekend."

They gave me a place to pitch my tent, and told me to dig a trench around it, and fill it with water so snakes could not get into my tent. What a joke! The place they gave me to pitch the tent was solid rock, and there was no way could I dig a hole around it, or even get the tent stakes in the ground, so I tied the tent to some trees. I was given no points towards that badge either. It seemed that I was not going to get many points that weekend, but just trying to survive seemed more important to me than points, at the time.

We were all trying to get the cooking badge, but who in their right mind could eat food that was filled with sand and dirt, then half-cooked over a fire? It was dreadful. Fortunately, I had brought some Pepsi-Cola and cookies along, so that's what I lived on for that weekend. I don't think I ever got a cooking badge. I did not know how to cook, anyway, so it did not make much difference to me. It was no wonder that when I eventually got home, mother said I seemed very hungry. A good meal at home really did taste great after that.

One other Boy Scout trauma happened when some older scouts wanted to take me for a fourteen-mile hike—seven miles into the country, and seven miles to return home. It was a cold, wet spring day, not really pleasant for hiking, and we were out to earn another merit badge. The older boys were really into the whole idea, but I wasn't. After we had walked the first seven miles into the country, the older boys choose a place for us to build a fire right beside a creek. They found some vines that we could swing across the creek on, and it seemed like great fun—'til one of the older scouts swung out, lost his grip, and fell into the creek.

He thought it was no big deal, since he could now show me how to dry clothes over the fire. This looked really great until I tripped over the sticks that were holding his clothes, and the whole mess fell into the fire. By the time we got the clothes out, half of them were burned up, and it was not a great day to be poorly dressed. We hurried back to town, and some nice lady driving by felt so sorry for the boy with so few clothes on, she offered us a ride home. Thank heaven for angels! I got the feeling that these scouts were not about to go hiking with me again, and I can say thank God for that. I had enough of the camping thing that one time. I ended up being given the merit badge, but I don't think that the older boys were too thrilled with the whole thing.

When I was a little older, one Christmas we celebrated up in the mountains of North Carolina. That would have been in the late '30s, when it was very much still backcountry. My mother was not really happy about the location, but was trying to deal with it in a mature fashion. Here we were, two young boys who didn't understand the lifestyle or the things that children did in the mountains, wondering about Christmas. I do remember that my mother and father bought wonderful presents for all of the less-fortunate children up in the mountain town. They wrapped them all up, and we took with us the most incredible Christmas tree. My mother had invited all of these little children up to our house, and most of them had never even seen a Christmas tree. She even had a little package for every one of them.

On Christmas morning, when I was opening my presents, I found that I always got way too much stuff. When we went back into the woods behind our place to see what "Santee" Claus had brought to these little mountain children, I was shocked. When I came back home, my mother said, "What's wrong?" I told her that I was upset because Santa Claus must have really hated the mountain children: They only got one present. I thought they must have been really terrible children during the year. One of them got a dime; one of them got a plastic comb. I sort of laugh about it now, because how do you explain to a child that it was because their family was poor. As a spoiled little kid who got everything, I just couldn't grasp how Santa Claus could have been so mean to them.

When I was with the mountain children, I learned a lot of new words and sayings. My mother was somewhat of a perfectionist about vocabulary and grammar, so she was quick to correct me when I began using the word, "yonder." I would say, "Mother, I'm going over yonder to see Billy."

Mother would reply, "You are going over *there* to see Billy."

After a church service one Sunday, she asked me about the sermon. I told her the preacher said, "Women have such long tongues, they can stand on the front porch, and lick slop out of the slop buckets on the back porch." Mother let me know gently that I was not to repeat that or use the word "slop," but she never put those folks down.

School, for me, was a real creative outlet. I attended Ravenscroft, which was a private school in Raleigh, and was part of Christ Church. It must have been new, as the classes were very small when I attended, and there were only twelve children in my entire class. Even at school, I could always find ways to stir things up and would do it just to drive people wild. They didn't realize that I was a boy with lots of ideas, and I did not always agree with their way of doing things. One good example of this is how I behaved in a common schoolyard situation:

A young Randy Trull stands apart from his small class at Ravenscroft School.

23

Randy stands front row, left, in this photo of Christ Church Boys' Choir.

Mother and Dad had given me a little ruby ring, which, to me, was just like a gift from God, since ruby is my birthstone. One day after school, I wanted to play out in the school yard, and I put my ring in my book bag and went off to play. When I returned, the ring was gone, and I did just what I thought I should do: I went straight to the police station and told them that this very valuable ring had been stolen at Ravenscroft. They listened very closely, and then put an advertisement about it in the newspaper. To say the school was a little upset is putting it mildly, and my parents asked me to tell them first before I told the world next time, as it would make everyone's life a little easier. This spoiled, cute, little boy turned out to be quite a handful!

Mother treated me as though I were made of gold. I am not sure that I was really as great as my mother thought I was, but who cares—she treated me like I was something straight from heaven. What kid wouldn't have liked that? As a boy I had very pretty, curly blond hair and blue eyes. As it turned out, I also had an exceptional little singing voice. I sang in the church choir at Christ Church, right on Capital Square.

My family was part of the membership of the Tabernacle Baptist Church, so I would go to Sunday school there, and then leave to go sing in the choir at Christ Church, which was Episcopalian and associated with Ravenscroft. I don't remember very much about it, but I must have had a beautiful voice and a very good memory for words. My mother also took me around to sing at all sorts of functions at different places and times. It was certainly something that she was proud of, just as anyone else's parent would be. As a kid, I got a big kick out of it!

One night I sang a solo at Tabernacle Baptist Church. I was upstairs in the choir loft all by myself, except for the organist. There was a bright light shining on me that made me a bit nervous. I sang the first verse of the song twice, but that was a rare thing. As a pushy kid, usually I was comfortable in the spotlight. Through it all, I did grow up a little. My nice treble voice went the way all boys go when they hit puberty—to hell in a hand basket—so my great singing career was over.

Mother's creativity comes to mind when I think of the '30s. My mother had made two little sharkskin suits for my brother and me. I think that they were for Easter, but I am not really sure. I only know she worked hard on them. My brother went running around and ended up in a briar patch. He tore his suit to shreds in there. I thought my mother was going to go ballistic when she saw what he had done to the outfit, but she always managed to deal pretty calmly with

Above: Randy couldn't help but add some giltz to the usual 1930s doll-house scene. Below: True designers usually start early. This "architectural rendering" is one of at least eleven such drawings that Randy made during his childhood. All the drawings featured window treatments, and for each exterior image, he included a floor plan.

our little antics. All in all, I have great memories of my early childhood days.

During these early years, I showed a tendency towards being creative with even small details in life. At one point, I put together an entire miniature apartment in my mother's spare pantry closet. I used the various shelves as though these were individual apartments, and each level was different, as were many of the rooms themselves. I used doll furniture, and completely furnished it with all the items I could imagine someone needing or wanting. I even went to the extent of covering several of the pieces with the silver foil from inside my mother's boxes of Camel cigarettes. She never knew what I was doing, but I carefully removed the liner and kept it smooth to make a perfect covering. I just recently found that mother saved these little mementos in a box, and I have them now. I suppose this was, in some form, foreshadowing my creative ability, and may have ultimately led me to my profession.

3 | *Growing up in the Forties*

AFTER WORLD WAR II came along in 1941, the most fun we had as kids was running up and down the street at night gathering information to tell the air raid people. We would tell them things like, "Mrs. Jones has light coming through her black-out curtains. You better get her straightened out." This would cause the air raid folks to fuss at Mrs. Jones, much to our delight.

Gas was rationed during the war, so we walked to Needham Broughton High School. New car production was shut down, too, and, often, there were only three or four cars in the school parking lot. They were all clunkers and barely ran. Mother and Dad bought bicycles so they could go to the golf course.

When Dad repaired commercial heating plants during the war, the customers would try to pay in kind. They would give him things, like food that he could not get at the time, but that didn't work out so well, either. Most of the food they gave us came in huge commercial-size cans, and we simply could not eat a whole gallon of pork and beans. Dad planted a Victory Garden across the street from our house, but we never got much produce from that little project.

One day, Dad fixed the heating unit in a ladies' clothing store. Hosiery was rationed and very expensive during those years, so they decided to pay him with nylons. Mother seldom complained about conditions during the war, but when Dad came home with new hosiery for her, she was one happy woman!

I am sure there were times when my parents really worried about the war, but it was fun and games to me. As I said, I didn't think much about the outside world. My friends and I just played war and pretended we were doing great things. Looking back, I don't think Raleigh was high on the Germans' bombing list, but what the hell—tattling on the neighbors was so much fun. World War II ended shortly before I turned sixteen. What a nice birthday present! Suddenly, there was plenty of gas, better cars, and all kinds of good food.

I headed off to high school in the eighth grade, because when I attended Ravenscroft, it was only a primary school, with first through seventh grades. This was before junior high school existed in our nation, and you began college by age sixteen. What a surprise it was to me when I arrived in Needham Broughton High School and found out that there were at least a hundred kids in my class. At Ravenscroft, I was used to so few students that the teacher could really watch us, but now I could have a ball.

I was not a very good student then, but I don't think it was because I lacked intelligence. It was that I simply wasn't interested in what they were teaching me, so I'd would just slide along and hope for the best. When I was in tenth

Randy Trull

Left: Randy attended handsome Needham Broughton High School in Raleigh where he made many contacts, both good business connections and warm friendships.

Right: This photo says it all: This high school relationship is doomed.

Above: Monk Trull, a fine amateur photographer, took this photo of Randy's high school girlfriend, Betty Robinson, and developed it in his dark room. Mabel Trull provided the tinting.

Right: Randy was an escort when Thomasville residents Martha Curlee (Vann) and Emily Finch (Lambeth) made thier debut in Raleigh, in 1951. All three are still good friends.

grade, I was voted the class clown, and the most congenial. I considered this a rather large compliment. I did put a lot of effort into those things that had interest for me, however. One of the things that made the teacher sit up and look a little surprised by was when she asked us to put together a pressed flower book, and to name the flowers. I really got into this idea.

I went out to the cemetery with some buddies, climbed over the fence, and picked flowers from all the beautiful arrangements on different graves. What a book I had! She said I must know someone in the flower business, since she had never seen so many cultivated varieties in a student's book. I think that she really meant for us to use wild flowers for our project, but what she never realized was that she was dealing a kid that looked at things differently, and went beyond the normal thought pattern of most kids.

Some years later, I got my driver's license and was pushing the limits. As soon as I could drive, I began thinking of getting out of Raleigh. It seemed smaller and smaller. I dreamed of living in a bigger world and tried to think how I would conquer it. I guess I drove my family crazy during that time.

I remember that I was out driving my father's car with some friends one night, and we got into trouble. We had an old, black '39 Dodge four-door sedan, and we were out on St. Mary's Street in the middle of the night. Because the road was slick from the recent rain, the car slid, and we hit a mailbox storage unit. It put a great big L-shaped dent in the front left fender. I was mortified, since it was Dad's car, so I had to figure out what to do.

My friends and I went to an all-night mechanic's shop and had the dent pounded out, and then sanded back into shape.

The only problem was that you could still see the mark in the paint. I came up with the bright idea of using black shoe polish to polish the whole fender. That worked fine until next time it rained. You should have seen the look on my father's face when he looked outside and saw the paint run off his car onto the ground! Even he had to laugh when I told him what had happened.

In about 1943, we moved out of town to a larger piece of property my father had bought. My father had the idea that it was important for us to be close to the land, so the country was the place to be. He really had no idea what this meant, since he had not grown up in that sort of environment, but that did not stop him. He had determined that this was the way it would be. He found an older house that he could work with, and even made the house heating system out of radiators that had been taken from a closed wing at the North Carolina State Mental Hospital. I'm not sure whether that was clever or strange, but that was one example of how he went about things.

One of the first things my father did when he moved out into the country was to buy a whole bunch of chickens. This was kind of ironic, since he didn't know anything about chickens, and my mother certainly did not care to learn. Not too long after this, my father went out of town with his best friend, Roland Nash. Mr. Nash owned the Dodge dealership and Daddy helped him deliver some cars back to Raleigh. While my father was gone, Mother had the chickens put to rest. When he returned home, and discovered they were gone, he informed my mother that someone had stolen his chickens. She said that they were outside in the ice cream box (what we used before frozen food lockers). My mother had gotten one of those old ice cream boxes from a grocery

Seven Gables at Creedmore was Randy's first school of antiques.

store, and she had all of the chickens cleaned and stored in it. As she explained to my father, "I'm not a farmer's wife. I am a lady, and I am not into chickens." With that said, she loaded a cigarette into her ivory holder, and went into the house.

We were city people, living in the country, and this had happened pretty suddenly. My mother was not into it at all, as she considered herself a lady—not a country wife. Because of this, she got in the habit of pulling the car up close to the house so she could get out and go directly inside. This prevented her from having to deal with the mud, animals, or other things about country life that did not please her.

Not long after we had settled in, we were having brunch at the country club and someone commented that Mother should get involved in the garden club since she had such a nice piece of property now. This made no sense, because she was definitely not into gardening, but it somehow piqued her interest. She said that she was not interested in plants, but she later admitted that she did like getting all dressed up and going to those ladies club meetings. She ended up becoming a member of several organizations like the D.A.R., and eventually became a Magna Carta Dame who went to England to celebrate the 750th signing of the document.

When we moved to the country, my father had bought every piece of equipment available, because his intent was to become a gentleman farmer. He knew absolutely nothing about farming, and that equipment was a disaster. The first thing he bought was an International Harvester tractor, with great big steel spikes on the wheels. My mother wouldn't even let him move it when my brother and I were at home because she was afraid that he might run us over.

"That clock was one of my parents' wedding gifts. The paneling in that house was beautiful," said Randy. (The *News and Observer*. Courtesy of NC Dept. of Cultural Resources)

Whenever he drove it on the highway, he would have to put boards down on the road so it wouldn't punch holes in the highway. That was typical of my father as he went through the farming episode: Act first, think later.

While he was in this stage of life, he would get many of the professors from N.C. State University to come out and tell him how to plant things that would help save the land by not using too many nutrients. They had many brilliant ideas for how to grow things. They showed him how to grow potatoes the size of watermelons, but nobody wanted them because they were too big. The only place that even had a machine big enough to cut them up was the state mental institution, so he gave that entire crop to them.

My father thought my brother and I should learn all about farming, so he gave each of us an acre of land, and told us to decide what we should grow there, and get to it. My brother, being the show off that he was, went out and planted a row of string beans and a row of potatoes. He was working out there in the hot sun, and I thought that was the pits, so I went through a plant book to help me decide the easiest thing to plant. I found out that you could plant radishes, and they would grow by themselves. I bought enough seeds to plant an acre, and just threw the seeds around.

Sure enough, they came up, and we had an acre of radishes. It wasn't because I wanted to; it was because my father made me. He said that if you were foolish enough to plant an acre, then you would have enough to last an entire lifetime. My father was really upset about this, and he said that since I planted them, I would have to pull them all up. The problem was, there were thousands of them! The only good part about that radish story is because I had to pull them all up, I had to do something with them. I sold them at the city market and made some money. It shouldn't be too surprising that I have never eaten a radish since then, and I hate them.

We went through these farming episodes, one after another, but not with very much success. We were a family, however, and we did things together. Most of the time, we even enjoyed it.

Since we were out in the country now, my father bought me a pony, and I named him, "Fellah." Fellah was just wonderful, and he loved for me to ride him. We could go any place that I wanted to go. When anyone else would get on him, all he would do is stand there and throw his back legs into the air. That made my father furious because all of his friends would bring their kids out to ride the pony, and Fellah would not want to go with anyone but me. My father was ready to do away with that pony, it made him so mad,

Randy concocted ways to avoid farming chores, but he never lost his love for the family's country home.

The barn at the Trull's country home provided Randy with a lofty getaway. "They stored hay upstairs and that's where we played when I was supposed to be working."

but I loved him and he loved me, so Dad let him be. We had a wonderful time together.

At this age and stage, I was always up to something. I don't mean that I was getting into trouble, but the things I came up with were pretty elaborate, and might even be seen as eccentric. A particular example here was that I would design an entire village in the woods behind our house — streets, houses, cars and everything. When I felt like one was finished with enough detail to suit me, I would simply start another. I just had the need to be busy, and to make things orderly.

Mother had enjoyed running the Raleigh silver and china shop she bought in 1930, and she still had a yen for that kind of thing. She began dabbling in buying and selling home furnishings out of our home during the early 1940s, but my father did not like all the people trafficking through the house. He was in bed one night, sitting up listening to the radio, when several customers walked right into "his space" to look at a piece of furniture. He said, "This is history," and built a seven-room cinder block house in the back yard for Mother to use as an antique shop.

When the end of World War II was in sight, she began stocking lots of inventory. Mother and my Aunt Pauline would drive to Pennsylvania to do their buying in places that were off the beaten path. There was not much furniture made during the war, and she knew people would soon be buying antiques again. Money would be flowing and customers would be looking for nice pieces to add to their homes.

Eventually, she made this storefront into a nice business, and called it the Seven Gables Antique Shop, after our house. She had a good reputation, and understood how to buy respectable antiques in lots, get rid of the junk, and make a profit off the good furniture. It was obvious always that Mother had great style, but her business abilities surprised even me at times. She was a born salesman, and knew how to make the numbers work.

I was in high school from 1944 until 1948, and I remember those years very well. It was a conservative place in the 1940s, but I was always stirring things up for my fellow students. I was pretty inventive, and into creating projects for myself. I'm not sure I was ever really very popular, though. I had friends, but I was not in the center of things at school. I was just one more kid in a school full of kids, and making passing grades was more than enough to keep me happy. I think that it was good enough to keep the family off of my

Randy designed the pep rally hood and hubcap covers for his parents' car. His creative approach to spelling is evident, too.

back, too, since I don't remember getting any hassle from them. I was always into original projects, like the complete towns I created in the woods near home, or the projects in the mother's antique shop. I guess I was more interested in getting out and around and seeing whatever the world had to offer me. Whatever opportunities were out there, I was much more interested in moving forward than just hanging around school.

When I was learning to drive, I remember wanting to drive fast most of all. I remember riding around in my Dad's car one night, and deciding to race against my friend, Thad Eure. We were zooming around in the Country Club Hills neighborhood in our respective cars, and he rounded the curb too closely. He hit a telephone pole, and tore up his Dad's Buick pretty badly right by Dr. Pascal's house. I had a camera with me and took pictures of the wreck. For some reason, we got the bright idea to take these down to the newspaper office and try to get them published.

As we hustled off towards downtown to the newspaper, I got picked up for speeding. That was when I learned that the law is the law, and you can't change the rules as you go along. The judge ended up taking away my license for six months, and Dad would neither support me, nor go to court with me.

Fate has a way of helping you out at times, and this was one of them, but Thad and I never knew about it. His father was the North Carolina Secretary of State, and would not have benefitted from that sort of negative publicity about his son's behavior. For that matter, Thad might not have had the chance at ultimate success with his Angus Barn Restaurant, had he been indicted for wrecking a car in a nice neighborhood when he was so young.

After the judge took my license, I had no way to get to school from our farm, and my father had to hire someone to chauffeur me back and forth. This was Willie Brown, the old black fellow who worked around our country house, and became a real fixture in my life. I had no idea just how nice it was to have someone like that until years later.

We ended up having a grand old time driving together, even though I did talk him into some trips that my father would definitely not have approved of, especially considering where we went and what we did. I somehow convinced Willie to pick up all the girls I liked, and to carry them to school. This really didn't sit well with my father, considering the fact that I was the one who lost his license, and this was supposed to be something of a punishment.

One particularly bright point from my high school days was when I dated a super nice gal. I think that Betty Robinson was one of the great crushes of my life. We had a lot in common, and I guess life proves that to you as you move along. She actually dumped me for somebody else. I should have fought for her, but that is history now.

Ironically enough, I ended up in interiors and home furnishings, and Betty ended up running a home furnishings store in North Carolina. I guess we did have a lot in common, but I did not realize how very much until later. Betty and her husband, Marion, attended my birthday parties when I turned seventy and seventy-eight. They dressed in "flap" clothes for the 2008 party, and we all had some big laughs together.

In the fall of 1948, I headed off to Campbell College, then a Baptist junior college, that combined two years of high school and two years of college. I think most of the students thought they might be preachers, so when they left

Campbell after two years, they went to Wake Forest to get their degrees in theology. Unlike these students, I went to Campbell just to finish what I started in high school, and did not have any idea where, or what, I would be doing when I graduated. As usual with me, I had a million ideas in my head those changed on virtually a daily basis.

School there was pretty normal for me, but I did have to preach one night at the church, though. I did not read very well, and so I thought that if I had some props to help me through, it would be easier for me. I took a bag full of knives up to the podium, and just kept pulling them out of the bag, using them to make points. I pointed to one as I spoke, and said, "You see, this is just like some of your lives. It is dull and has no point or direction!" After my speech that evening, my religion teacher said that he was quite sure no one slept through my talk, but he did wonder if preaching was the right thing for me.

We had a choir at Campbell, and I sang with them. On

"Guess who's coming to dinner?"—the entire Campbell College Choir.

one occasion, they were going to sing at our church in Raleigh, at the Tabernacle Baptist church. Since Campbell was just thirty-two miles from our house, I came home all the time, but my father said I should stay at the school more as he was paying for the food and I was eating at home too much. I ate way too much to suit him, anyway. I asked my mother if I could have some of my choir friends come for dinner the night we sang at our church. Dad put in his two cents: "How many, and do they eat like you?" But Mother's response, of course, was "yes," and every week or so after that, I asked her again. Each time the number got a little bit bigger, and two weeks before the event, I told her that I had asked twelve friends. My father went wild, but Mother seemed okay with it.

The week before we were to come over, Mother asked me again, "Are you sure that there will just be twelve?"

I took a big breath, and said, "To tell the truth, I was having a hard time just asking certain ones, so I invited the entire choir for dinner."

Man, my father came up out of his chair fast, and looked at me with fire coming out of his eyes. He demanded, "How many is that?"

I just smiled and said, "Fifty-three."

He flew out the door, and I am sure the neighbors could hear him using all those ugly words. Mother, always the dear, just said, "Fine: We will deal with this, and it will not be that bad."

The day of the dinner, mother had all her friends out to the house to help her prepare. They made a huge chicken salad in the punch bowl. She realized that with that many kids coming, the only way to handle the situation was for her to have extra tables and chairs. That way, when they arrived, she would just tell them to sit down at a table, and dinner would already be served.

Dad had to go to the funeral home and rent chairs and tables, so he really looked out of sorts when the bus pulled up in front of our house. We put tables in every room of the house so that no one could walk around with the food, and mother's friends helped her make sure everyone got fed. It went off great, and I think Dad got over it later. Today, I still do like to entertain, even if it is a crowd.

Not a lot went on at Campbell that I thought was very exciting, except that they let me be the set designer for a play that we were putting on. I designed the most handsome set, most of it with furniture from our house. I thought no one would care, as we only needed it for one night, and mother and father were going to be out of town. Things went great until my parents came home early, found over half of the living furniture missing, and called me. Dad went a little wild and rushed down to the school. Mother convinced him to let it stay in the set until the show was over. He agreed, but would not leave school unless all the furniture was back on a truck, heading to Raleigh. He just didn't have a sense of humor about some of my fabulous ideas.

My link to Raleigh and the old country place was strong, even as I lived and worked in New York years later. The house was really something special, and when I would come home, years later, it was still like living in the country. After my mother's death, for a long time the house just sat there, and it was a very tempting place for people to break into. Even though I had a security system installed, at one point someone did break in, and I had to go down and check on the damage. Once there, the sheriff asked me all sorts of questions for the police record.

He looked out in the yard, noticed someone moving around, and asked, "Who is the black gentleman in the yard?"

Without thinking about it, I said "Willie."

He then asked, "What is his last name?"

I looked at him and said, "I really don't know. He just came with the house."

It is safe to say that the sheriff looked dumbfounded as I tried to make him understand that Willie had been there since I was a child, and I had no prejudice towards the man. I just took his presence for granted.

He was almost like a member of the family, but to my knowledge, I had never heard his last name spoken. My father had taken good care of Willie, and found him an apartment in a retirement home when he got to be too old to live by himself. Daddy would go see Willie and sometimes he would bring him out to see the house and garden. He would just sit there, as it was as much home to him as anywhere else. By the time he died, I had found out his full name. I had "Willie Brown" carved into his grave marker.

4 | *Living It Up in the Fifties*

WHEN I GRADUATED from Campbell Jr. College in January of 1950, I had my sights set on Rollins College in Florida. I had heard that it was like a big country club. You could even take water skiing and sailing courses there, and I thought that sounded very much like something I might enjoy.

Unfortunately, around that same time, Dad went to one of his Lion's Club lunches and found out more than I wanted him to know about my new school. He was talking with a friend of his and said, proudly, "My son is going to Rollins College."

The man laughed and told him, "That's a first class country club, but your son should enjoy it."

Later that day, my father came home and announced that there were a lot of places that I was going, but Rollins was not one of them.

A friend of my mother's suggested that I might like to go to Parsons School of Design in New York. I had always been interested in fabrics, textures, wallpaper, and furniture, so it sounded pretty good to me. My mother called Parsons, got me registered, and arranged my trip to New York City.

Leaving home to go to school in New York—at the age of nineteen—certainly marked a profound change in my life. I'm not sure that I even realized that when I stepped on the train in Raleigh. In seemed in that one instant, I'd become a man. No Mother and Dad to turn to now—just me and that big city. New York would be a long way from Raleigh.

I had on a nice felt hat, a lined overcoat, and carried handsome luggage. I came into New York at Pennsylvania Station, and was immediately awed. My father, who had friends at the YMCA in Raleigh, had called the Y on 34th Street in Manhattan to make sure that they would take care of me and help me find a more permanent place to stay. In the meantime, I would stay there. My parents thought this would make my arrival easier, as I could just walk straight from the station and check into my room.

Before I could get to the safety of the YMCA, and my room, the wind took my handsome gray felt hat right off my head and flipped it into the gutter, where it landed squarely in a mud puddle. That was the end of that hat, my very first day. It was a bit dramatic start, to say the very least.

I was given a room about the size of a postage stamp, and that presented me with quite a problem. I had brought enough trunks of clothes that when I unpacked, I almost had to sit out in the hall. I also had no idea about where to go, or how to get places, so it took me two days to find the school. When I finally did, everyone looked at me like I was a foreigner, and I don't guess that they thought much of the southern accent. One of them even asked me if I was an American.

I was only nineteen when I went to Parsons, and that made me one of the youngest students in the class. The guy who was actually the youngest, Matthew Sergio, was only six months younger than me, and was probably a little smarter—much more of a city boy than me. He was born in New York City, but his parents were native Italian. His father had passed away and he lived with his mother and three sisters in Astoria, out on Long Island. We became great friends in school, and I thought that it was odd that he never asked me to his home. That's probably the first thing I would have done if he was in my hometown, but maybe that's just a Southern thing.

If you asked Matthew, he would tell you that I talk all the time, and that he can hardly get a word in edgewise. The truth is that we both talk a lot, and I think he talks more than I do, but I am sure he would not agree. While at school, I must have talked too much about my life in North Carolina, and about going to the country club, and other things that made me seem spoiled (which I was). I think he thought that I would not like the fact that he and his mother, and his three sisters, lived on the second floor of a walk-up in Astoria. He finally did invite me to come out for dinner, though.

Young Randy made this shirt himself because he wanted the pattern to "line up just right."

What a great evening it was. They treated me like I was part of the family, but the only problem was that when I said something to his mother in English, she would say something to

Matthew in Italian. I later found out that she could not understand Southern English, so she would have to ask him what I had said. I learned to talk a little more "Northern," and she was able to understand me a little better. Now, fifty years later, I am still a remote part of his family, and he is still one of my best friends. We don't agree on much of anything except that we are still around, and ready to argue over just about anything. When we are not together, he will stand up for me, and I will do the same for him. And what a crazy world it is—we both ended up living up in North Carolina.

I could tell you that I was really a great student, but the truth is that I drove the teachers mad. They finally put me in the back of the room, in hopes that I would not create more problems. Leave it to me, however, to go along and do something unusual, even by accident.

One day, I dropped a tube of purple paint on the floor, stumbled as I went to pick it up, and firmly stepped on it. Into the air squirted the purple goo, covering nearly the span of the entire classroom. Most of it landed on a girl sitting in the front of the class, who had just stretched a piece of paper on the board, and was waiting for it to dry. Suddenly, the paper was purple, and I wondered why. I saw the line of paint going up front, but had no idea that I had caused it until I noticed the tube on the floor. After this, the word went out to faculty and students that there was no place to get away from me.

They probably didn't think much of my flannel shirts and dungarees, either. They were all dressed in the latest styles. It took me a while to understand all of that. At the beginning, I had such a rough time, especially since I was so used to being spoiled by my family. Here I was on my own in New York City, trying to find a place to live, and no one was very friendly.

The most amazing thing to me was that everybody was asking me for references, and since I wasn't from there, I had none. After all, when you come from a small town in the South, everyone knows everyone. You never even hear the word "references" because people either know your people, or they don't trust you (simple). Then suddenly, you are in this great big city and everybody is asking the same question, "Who are your references?"

It began to snow. I was cold, and I was lonely. I really must say that in those first few weeks, I hated New York with a passion. I think that I might have gone home except for the fact that I remember my father saying, "Don't worry, he'll be home in a week," to my mother while we were standing at the train station. I was not going to give in that easily, and was determined to prove my father wrong about me.

I finally did see an advertisement in the paper for a little bedroom with a sitting room for rent, part of someone else's apartment. I went over to see the place on a cold, rainy day. When I got there, I sat and talked to a very proper lady named Mrs. Hood. She gave me this lecture: "This will be your room and you'll share the bath in our apartment. You can't have strangers in." She also went on to ask, "Who are your references?"

I looked at her and said, "Lady, I'll give you the governor of the State of North Carolina, both our senators, and all our congressmen, but I don't know anybody in this city!"

She took all my references down, and said, "I'll call you."

I had a horrible cold and felt terrible. When I went back to the Y, I just sat in my room, staring out the window. Then the phone rang. It was Mrs. Hood saying, "I would like to talk to you again. Could you come over?"

Prior to this, I had been sitting there looking out at the

weather thinking that I would do almost anything to get out of that cramped little room for the evening. Feeling doomed to my claustrophobic quarters made the hopelessness and my cold feel even worse. I went back to see her, hoping she would ask me some easy questions. When I arrived, she immediately saw how sick I was, and was apologetic because she had made me come out in that awful weather again. She made me tea, and made coffee for herself, then said, "You can move in tomorrow."

I moved in, and it was the most incredible experience. Here was a woman who obviously had a good education, and had come from a family with a great deal of money at one time, but who found herself in tough times now. Her husband had either gambled it away or had drunk it away. I don't know what had happened to it, but he had lost it all. She was left alone, and virtually destitute, in New York City after his death.

She was a very sophisticated, charming lady who just seemed to need some companionship. After her husband's death, she married a wallpaper hanger. He wasn't anybody of great class or style, but he was companionship for her at that point and time in her life. She had evidently had a very tough time living in New York alone before this, and wanted to banish the loneliness. After all, they had no children, this was his third marriage, and of course this was her second.

Mr. and Mrs. Hood practically adopted me. They enjoyed me because I was not accustomed to sitting alone in one room, and their sitting in another. I joined in their conversations, and one of the first things I did was to go to the refrigerator and inspect their food. Within a matter of a week, it was like I was their kid, and they were looking after me. I must say that my parents were thrilled when they called and asked Mrs. Hood questions about my whereabouts and Mrs. Hood answered them. She would say things like, "Well, he has gone out this evening and he won't be back until late. He is feeling fine, though." My mother felt like there was somebody in the big city watching out for me all the time.

I thoroughly enjoyed them. Her husband was a gas, and he took me to Coney Island sometimes. He showed me all of the rides because he had grown up out there, and we had a good time. It was like being home and having a family, and I certainly didn't anticipate something like that when I moved to New York. As time and the years moved on, my family became very friendly with them. Edith Hood became one of those very, very special people in my life.

Years later, Mr. Hood decided that they would move to Atlantic City. It was cheap and they could live close to the boardwalk, and they could get outdoors there because New York City was becoming a tough place to live. After they moved down there, I did not see them a lot, and he died after only a couple of years.

I enrolled at Parsons School of Design in New York City later that month. I was only there for eleven months the first time I attended, but I made a good start. I did not have a thought in my head about the fact that I was in the Naval Reserves, and was busy with school. The Korean War was just not on my list of things to do. When I came home for Christmas that year, the fact of the war's existence and my commitment to the Navy really set in: I was called up for active duty in December. Although it turned out that I never actually made it over there, the prospect of being sent was pretty shocking.

Although I joined in good faith and with good intentions, my personal conclusion was that the U.S. Navy was better off without me. I started in the Naval Reserves, but I was quickly called into active duty. My friend, Lamont Fitzgerald, and I went in together, and took a troop train from Raleigh, North Carolina to the Great Lakes Naval Center, just north of Chicago, in January. On an average winter's day there, it was twenty degrees below zero.

When the train arrived at the naval post, the ground was frozen solid. There was a big sign there when we arrived that said, "Welcome to the U.S. Navy." I looked up and thought, what a stupid sign, and then I fell on the ice and broke three ribs. They had to carry me on a stretcher just to get me through the gates, and that was the beginning of my career in the Navy! As soon as I got out of the hospital, they shaved my head, and a short time later, I caught pneumonia and my eyes became so swollen that I was put back in the hospital. I was eventually sent back to the barracks, but this time my forehead swelled up. Now I know that it was probably a sinus infection or something like that, but during this time in medical history, the doctors had fewer options of treatment. They used two steel tubes and crammed these up my nose to drain the fluids. My sinuses have never been right since that happened.

When I went into the Navy I was 6'1", 149 pounds; when I left boot camp, I was only 98 pounds! During my stay, a young doctor wanted to operate on my eyes, but I did not agree with him. He told me, "You had better go along with me or you will suffer during your time here," to which I replied, "You just threatened the wrong person!"

I made a call to my parents who came up through Washington, D.C. They made a particular stop there to see both Representative Harold Cooley and our senator, who

Military order and artistic impulses don't always mix well, but Randy did his patriotic duty nonetheless. He is pictured here with Navy friend Lamont Fitzgerald.

were friends of theirs, to see what could be done about my situation on the base. By the time they arrived, the doctor was driving me around in his private car. He didn't operate on me after all, and we got along just fine after that.

When I left the naval center, I was on another troop train, but they put me in a private cabin, as they were concerned about my health. They had to stop the train in West Virginia because I had a fever of 104 degrees. They brought a doctor aboard, and he gave me some pills. They couldn't treat me there because I was on military land, and the troop train went on to the Norfolk Naval Hospital, its final destination. When we arrived, they announced that everybody was going home on two weeks leave. I chose not to report to the military hospital as ordered, and went home instead.

My parents realized that I was ill and took me to Duke Hospital, where I was treated. I was pumped full of vitamins and antibiotics, and allowed to rest for four or five days. While in the hospital, my condition improved and I was able to return home. When I reported back for duty, I was better, but still not really healthy. One evening, I was headed across the base for home, and I walked right into a tree. I knew right then that something was wrong with my eyes.

I went back to Norfolk and was assigned to the Little Creek Amphibious Base. I was a very good typist, which led me to become an assistant to a Lieutenant, who ran the

Mabel Trull's concern for Randy's health is written on her face, but time has proven his constitution was sound.

commissary. For non-military readers, this is a store that is a combination of a grocery and department store. I was then reassigned to be in charge of the nursery at the commissary on post. Women were not allowed to bring their children into the commissary, so a nursery was provided. The women liked the way I cared for the children so much that they tipped me! In a short time, I was watching between eight and fifteen kids at a time, and I had saved enough money to put in two sandboxes, six swings, and two see-saws.

Since I had done this of my own accord, and with my own money (at no cost to the Navy or government), I was a great success until one of the local papers published a photo of me with the children. The article read something like "We are at war, but here is man spending his time watching children." That was the end of that! I was immediately transferred to the Recreation Department. So much for the Navy's being benevolent.

My next little venture was when I started a cheerleading squad for the football team. We even had our own special jerseys and everything. That didn't last too long, though, as the commanding officers decided to do away with the football team. This wasn't too surprising, considering that we were at war. To have some recreation in its place, I came up with the idea to have bingo one night a week.

I charged ten cents a card. With the money the games generated, I bought radios, wrist watches, and other fancy items to award as prizes. As word spread about the nicer prizes, the whole hall started to fill up every night. At one point, I had made two hundred dollars, all in dimes. Dimes!

I gave away a hundred dollars in prize money, and still had plenty left over to purchase the prizes themselves. I should note that during all of this time, I still had a physical problem with stamina and my eyes, but that the authorities in the Navy had not decided that it was important enough to put me in the hospital, so I soldiered on and kept busy.

As with any U.S. naval base, there were frequent inspections carried out by captains or admirals on our station as well. Every time the inspecting officer arrived, the band would strike up with the musical fanfare. Joking, I once said, "If that band strikes up one more time, I'll faint!" As that old saying goes, "You had better be careful what you wish for," because sure enough, I fainted not too long after that, and woke up in the ambulance.

A few weeks later they were having another inspection, and the lieutenant was concerned about me fainting again. He ordered me to stay in bed the day before the inspection, and they had an ambulance nearby during the inspection, just in case. As it turned out, this did little good. The captain stopped in front of me during the inspection, and I fell out, right into his arms! All in all, I spent one year and twenty-one days in the hospital during my career in the Navy. A note on the Navy's response here: My enlistment was about to expire, and the only way the Navy could even legally keep me in the service was to put me in the hospital.

After serving my time in the Navy, I was discharged in 1952, and returned to school in New York. I rented an apartment with Larry Robinson, who I had known from my first year at Parsons, and also managed to get a part-time job working retail in the eleven-story McCreery's Department Store at 34th Street and Fifth Avenue. I worked Monday and Thursday nights, and all day on Saturdays. The job taught me a lot about working with people. It was a good complement to what I was learning at Parsons at the same time.

McCreery's had been one of New York's fine high-end ladies' stores for fifty or sixty years. It was still a fine store when I worked there, too, but it went out of business unexpectedly in 1954. The building was sold to Ohrbach's.

When I went to work at McCreery's, they placed me in the adjustment department and told me that listening to complaints was the best way to learn the store. My supervisor was a lady named Hutchinson and I let her know I wanted to get out there and hustle. I wanted to be ahead of the pack. My father always told me, "You can be a little frog in a big pond, or a big frog in a little pond." I always told him I wanted to be a big frog and big pond, and that is what I tried to do in New York.

My first assignment was to work at a desk where I handled upholstery adjustments for the furniture department. The first call I took was from a lady who said she had bought a sofa from McCreery's and the springs were coming right through the cushions.

I said, "Well, that's terrible. Could you hold on, please, for a moment?"

So I turned to the old battle-axe who ran the upholstery section and said, "This lady bought a sofa here and the springs are coming right through the cushions."

She said, "When did she buy it?"

So, I asked the caller, "When did you buy the sofa?"

"Oh, about ten or twelve years ago," she answered.

The old battle-axe said, "Tell her to get lost! We don't fix anything after ten years." That was a very New York way to handle things. I tried not to be so abrupt, but I did learn to ask a lot of questions.

Since I was only working part-time, I had no specialty at McCreery's. Mrs. Hutchinson just put me where she needed me, and sometimes that sent me to work on the eight-man switchboard. The store ran ads in the newspaper for items that could be ordered by telephone. Someone would clip current ads and hang them on a chain that went all the way around the switchboard, so that we could see exactly which product the callers were referring to. One evening a lady called and she started discussing a dress that was on sale. I could see the dress in the newspaper clipping, so I asked her some things about her figure.

Finally, she asked, "Well, how do you think that dress will look on me?"

I answered, "Terrible." Suddenly, all the other operators plugged in to listen. They thought, "What in the world is he saying?"

I said, "We do have a dress that would look beautiful on you. It is a gorgeous dress, but it is not on sale. It's very stylish and I think this is the perfect dress for you."

She proceeded to order the dress, and after she had worn it several times, she wrote the store to say, "This is the most beautiful dress I have ever had. I have no idea who I was talking to, but he had a Southern accent."

Sometimes I worked at the general complaint desk. The office wall was wood half-way up and the upper section was a big window. There was always a long line of people who were waiting, and they could see me and the person I was talking to. I learned quickly that women who wore a size 6 or 8 dress would spend hundreds of dollars to look one-half size smaller, but a lady who wore a size 52 would only buy a $12.95 girdle, then return it saying, "It does nothing for me."

I was sitting at the adjustments desk one day when a lady who was a size 52 proceeded to try and pull her girdle up from her feet, then over her dress to show me it did nothing to make her look any slimmer. Everyone in line could see her. It was hysterical. It was like something out of a movie set. She grunted and pulled, grunted and pulled, but she was so large she just couldn't squeeze herself into it. Finally, I said, "I take your word for it."

By that time, she couldn't get the girdle to move up or down, so I finally pulled it off her by the hose-strap. Then, swinging it by the strap, I took the girdle to Mrs. Hutchinson and said, "What do I do with this thing?"

She said, "For heaven's sake — give her the $12.95 and get her out of the store."

I was still working at McCreery's when the announcement was made that it was closing. A lady came in one day and said, "I bought a chair here. I paid for it. The store delivered it, but they delivered the wrong chair. I like the chair they delivered, so I'm keeping it. I went upstairs and bought the same chair again that I wanted the first time. Again, you have delivered the wrong chair twice. I would like for you to deliver the chair I asked for."

The chair she really wanted was out of stock by that time. I tried to explain to her that the store was running in utter confusion, because we were in the process of going out of business. People were just tearing tags off, salesmen were confusing what was sold and what was not. So I told her, "Enjoy the chair you bought first and I'll give you a credit for your second purchase."

She said, "No, I want my chair."

This woman came in regularly. As fate would have it, one Saturday morning they announced that the store was closing officially at five o'clock that very same day. She was sitting in my office when they made the closing bell sounded. I said, "Madam, with the ringing of that bell, I'm out of a job, and you're out of a chair."

"Well, what am I going to do?" she asked.

I answered, "Like those famous words from *Gone With The Wind*, 'frankly, my dear, I don't give a damn.'" I walked out and left her sitting in my office.

Lord and Taylor, parent company to McCreery's at that time, took over the adjustments department. They asked me if I would work in the evenings, and I said, "Sure. As long as I don't have to face customers, I'll be happy to help you clean the place up." So, I worked there for a while, while my time at Parsons was winding down.

My parents did come to visit me several times while I was in school there, but Dad was really not much for the city. He chose to come up one time since there was some big parade for the Shriners, and he loved that sort of thing. While he and mother were in the city, I had a party for the kids in my class at my apartment on 67th Street and Madison Avenue. I told Mom and Dad that I had to go downtown to pick up my date for the evening, so I used Dad's car. He told me to be sure that I got back there before any of the kids arrived, as he and mother would not know them.

My luck wasn't so good that evening, and I had a flat tire. I knew I was going to be late getting back to the apartment, so I called to tell them what had happened, and that I would be there soon. Dad answered the phone, and proceeded to tell me that someone was sitting in the living room who was old enough to be my mother. He said that he had opened the door, and a lady was standing there in a full length mink coat, with a hat and a veil. Dad had a hard time accepting this, as my friends in New York were dressed to the nines, and he was expecting the sort of school kids he had known from Campbell. Since this was Parsons School of Design, they all dressed up every day.

When she said her name, he looked at her oddly because he was sure she was not coming to the party. It was Renee Vermont, a wonderful lady from Paris who decided to become an interior designer, and so she was in my class at Parsons. I had a really mixed group of friends, both because of Parsons itself, and due to my own outgoing personality.

I remember one day I was sitting at my desk in class, and began to feel funny. It was really warm in the center of the room. The students who were by the windows commented that they did not want the windows open because it got too cold. There were a lot of windows in the room, and I wanted to let some air in, so I walked up to the head of the class to speak with the teacher.

"Excuse me, Mr. Hadley. Do you think we could open the windows so we could get some air in here? It gets so stuffy in the middle of the classroom."

Mr. Hadley implied that he couldn't do much about it, but I wasn't satisfied, and thought there might be something I could do.

I left the room and went up to the office of the president of the school at the time, a very French and proper man. His secretary greeted me, "May I help you?"

"I'm Randy Trull," I said. "I'm downstairs in Interior Design, and I would like to speak to Mr. Bedouir."

She replied, "He is busy right now but I will ring you as soon as he is available."

When I walked back down the stairs every window in the room was open and everybody was laughing. They asked me, "Are you happy now, Randy?"

It was as cold as a refrigerator. When their little joke was over, they closed all the windows. The phone rang, and the secretary said, "Mr. Bedouir can see you now."

When I went back upstairs, he asked me, "What is the problem?"

I replied, "I can't understand that cow's ass that you have for a teacher."

The president almost dropped dead from shock and said, "What do you mean by a cow's ass?"

When I told him what had happened, he said, "Mr. Trull, I assure you that it will not happen again."

I said, "Thank you," and went back downstairs. About a week passed, and as I left the classroom, I passed Mr. Bedouir in the hall. Within earshot of my professor's classroom, I spoke loudly enough to make myself heard

I said, "Well, thank you! I really appreciate everything that YOU have done for me."

Mr. Hadley was so mortified by my sarcasm, and the fact that I had spoken to the president about this, that the rest of that winter, all of the windows were cracked during class. I guess he got my message.

There was one other eccentric teacher who is worth mentioning. His name was Mr. Guy, and he was head of the department. One day he said that we were to design a bachelor's beach house, and all of the students were working on it. Since this was in the early 1950s, things like television were not considered of major importance.

Mr. Guy was sitting there with his pencil, sketching away, and said, "I think that you should have a nice large sofa. I would like to have a large sofa in the room that I can lounge on."

I said to him, "Well, don't you think that the sofa is just a little bit large for the room?"

He replied, "Well, I would like to have a large sofa to spread all of my books over."

I said, "My God! How big could your books be?" After all, he had drawn a sofa that was twelve feet wide. I could see that he was becoming furious with my blunt questions, but that did not deter me.

The next thing he sketched in was a television set, and I said to him, "Do you think that people would really want a television in a beach house."

He said, "Of course!"

And, too soon, I said, "They don't even have decent programs on in the summertime—all that they have on are re-runs!"

Then he said, "You use this house twelve months a year."

After all this, I really did not know what to do with this house. In an attempt to do the assignment, I was sitting at my desk wondering what to do, so I drew a great big circle, right in the middle of the room.

Mr. Guy walked by and said, "What in the world is that?"

"It's a brewery," I replied, "the guy is an alcoholic."

I think that's the last word he ever said to me until I graduated. Evidently, I did do something right while I was there, because I won the Baker award for good design. He read my name out so quietly that I didn't even know that it was my name. I don't think he was too thrilled to find out that I had been voted the winner. I did manage to graduate from the school, but there were some really wild episodes. Looking back, I realize that I truly received a good education that has helped me a great deal as I have gone through life.

Bill Leonard was in my class at Parsons, and he was three years older than I, so to me, he was a much older guy. I thought he was a great fellow, but we were not really good friends, just schoolmates. In our third year, one day he walked over to my desk and said let's have dinner sometime. I liked the idea, and said sure.

At that point I was sharing an apartment with three other guys, and we really had a wild place, with lots of parties. The night Billy came over for drinks, all my roommates were out, and we just sat and talked. We then went out for dinner, and returned to the apartment for nightcaps. At this point, the phone rang, and it was one of my roommates telling me he was at a bar on 42nd Street.

They had run out of money, and needed me to come right down and help them out. It was after midnight, and Billy looked at me and laughed, "This is really a madhouse." I headed to the bar to pay the bill, and Billy went home.

When we graduated in May of 1954 and went to Europe, it turned out he and I were roommates on the ship, and later, in Europe. We became good friends then, and got to know each other well on that trip. We have been friends for life, almost like brothers.

My mother and father came back to New York for graduation, but Dad was not really a big fan of the city. He was sharp as a tack, but not into the wild sophistication of his son's world at Parsons. When they arrived in New York, they asked where the graduation would be with relation to the school's campus, and I responded that it would be in the Grand Ballroom of the Plaza Hotel.

Clearly shocked, my father said, "YOUR graduation is in the ballroom of the PLAZA hotel?"

"Of course," I replied. "Where else would the Parsons school of design be graduating?"

Anyway, the graduation was on a Friday, and all of us at

school were excited. There was a lot of packing going on, since there were twenty-six of us that were going to continue our schooling with a Parsons branch in Paris for a few months. After all, here we were graduating, then sailing to Europe on Saturday!

We were to set sail on the Ile de France, and that thrilled us, even thought we were to be berthed in the lowest class cabins that could be booked. I think we were below the water line, and I had high hopes of getting into the upper cabins.

I immediately made friends with one of the chefs in our dining room and asked him, "How can I get up to the better-class levels of cabins, if I want to go look around?"

He came back with a spoon, bent into an odd shape, and said, "If you use this, it will unlock every door in the place."

The first night, I rushed back from dinner, put on my evening clothes, grabbed my "key," and headed upstairs to see what the action would be in each class. In cabin class, it was really lively, because there was a party going on in a beautiful lounge. The scene in first class was very dull, though. So, I decided to make this into a little social mixing business. I took people from first to cabin, and friends from economy to cabin, so that cabin became the fun place for everyone. From then on, I was taking everyone from class to class, and the middle class became the hot lounge—everyone wanted to be there.

We all had a ball on that trip! When we actually arrived in Paris, we were there early. We had quite a bit of time to explore the city, since school wasn't starting for another ten days. I had some friends who were also going to be there on holiday, so four of us got together and decided that we were going to drive to North Africa. We had no idea of the distance, or how we were going to do this, but it seemed like a fun idea. We were going to go to Tangier, which was in Morocco. It was an international city and considered wild and exciting.

The cheapest car we could get was a little Renault, and it had a tiny engine in the back. There were four of us, and we decided we were only going to take two suitcases. We put one suitcase up in the front of the car and strapped the other on top of the car. We took off from Paris and traveled through Biarritz to Spain. You have to remember this was in 1954, and Spain didn't even have a highway patrol, so we were pretty much on our own if something went wrong.

We had a wonderful trip, though, and at one point we stopped at a grocery store to get some food. Oddly enough, this place had a crystal chandelier. I really wanted to buy it, so I negotiated with the owner. After we struck a deal, we boxed the chandelier and put it on top of the car, next to the suitcases. We took it all the way down to Algiers with us, and proceeded to get on a boat.

We took the boat to Tangier, which was such an international and mysterious city. We drove to Torremolinos, which is a grand resort, even today. When we got there, there were no hotels, just beaches and a private house. You had to walk down this cliff to get to the beach. Today that is considered the Riviera of Spain. We drove through Spain, and, on our way back to Paris, we decided to go through the Alps.

There was a lot of snow up on the mountains, and when we went to cross the border, they didn't even know what to do with us. They probably had very few Americans pass through, much less four nutty ones like us. It was remote enough that the check point just had a big stick stuck across the road. The guards finally let us pass.

It was all very exciting; we were young, and full of our-selves, discovering all sorts of things. We had a great trip, and got back to Paris just in time to start school.

Lots of crazy things went on in Paris, but I as I think back, only a few stood out that seemed amusing enough to include here. Van Day Truex, our instructor, was a fabulous person, and he had such style. He was president of Parsons for a few years and, eventually, became director of design for Tiffany's.

One day, I was talking to him out in front of Versailles. I said to him that I understood that when we got to Italy, we could buy suits really cheaply.

He looked at me and said, "Oh yes! Half of what you could get them made for in New York. Why, they only cost four to five hundred dollars!"

I thought he was mad, so I tried to change the subject and said I gathered you could have shoes made for next to nothing, too.

He smiled again, and said "Oh yes, just eighty or ninety dollars."

I told him that was what I paid for suits, and I was hoping that I could get them made for half that. He laughed, and wished me good luck. You must remember that this was 1954, and ninety dollars to a kid in school was a fortune. On top of that, I had never really paid for anything since I could turn to my Dad and say, "Here's the bill." I told you I was lucky!

I shared a room with Bill Leonard. He had a really crazy mother, and she wrote him letters all the time, telling him things to buy for her. Her list of Parisian perfumes would have broken the bank, but the things that she wanted from Italy really got me. She wrote to tell him if he saw a really nice mantelpiece, pick one up for her. Did she think we were traveling with a moving van? By the time school was over, and we were in Milan, we did need a moving van and more money just to get home.

I told Bill that I was afraid that my father was going to tell me to swim home, but Bill said "Ask your parents for five hundred dollars. If they send you two, you will be fine." I did that, and I got a letter from them. At first, I was afraid to open it as I thought, "Lord God, I'm going to have to swim home." I finally sat down, opened the letter, and luckily my mother said she had sent me five hundred dollars, although she could not imagine what I needed it for. Man, that was great! I dashed off to London, stayed at the Ritz, of course, and arrived back in New York, broke. Dad was a more than a little bent out of shape, but what the hell, I had a great trip.

The school had told our parents how much money we would need to be able to live in Paris and to go to school. Of course, you can imagine how that went with me: I went through the cash in about six weeks. I didn't really worry about it because my mother was coming to visit me during the first several weeks, and she would have plenty of money. If I was going to be bankrupt by the time she arrived, it really didn't matter because I knew that she wouldn't let me starve for the rest of the school session.

There are always those things that happened in school that stick in our memories, and one of these comes to mind when I think back to those days. Our teacher was a man named Mr. Barrows, and he was a really incredible person, and a wonderful teacher. He knew the history of France and Italy in detail, and also exposed us to the most intimate and interesting parts of the design field. He really man-

The Parsons students take a break inside the Coliseum in Rome, 1954. "The instructor (second from right) was Italian and very sharp," said Randy. "Jack Lamb (far left), of Wilson, NC, was a good friend."

Randy and Dr. Forest P. Clay met by chance in Paris, in 1954. Later. when Pat taught physics at Rutgers, he became Randy's roommate on Third Avenue. "Randy used the apartment in numerous promotions," Clay said in 2009. "There was always something going on."

aged to integrate aspects of both history and design into our studies.

He took us to Versailles and other such museums and locations. His ability to make the location live, and be relevant, to us, as students, turned out to be of great importance to us as we progressed and absorbed it all. The Parsons connection was really helpful, and allowed us access to some really fantastic homes.

Randy and Bill Leonard are pictured here in Siena, Italy. "He decided to peroxide his hair and I think he added some Clorox. By the time he got through, there was smoke coming off the top of his head," described Randy.

Some of the things he could tell us were really story book tales. For young kids like us, Mr. Truex was like an idol and we all wanted to be like him. He had superb taste, class, and style. While we were there, he invited us to a premier designer's home for a cocktail party. Mr. Truex convinced Mr. Frank to give the party for the students, so we arrived all dressed up, and there we were, being entertained by the leading designers.

We were sitting there drinking champagne, and Mr. Truex said to us, "Why doesn't each of you introduce yourself to Jacques Fran."

I put out my hand and said, "I'm Randolph Trull," and the next person said, "I'm Roy Richters." This went on until it reached a little Italian boy from Bridgeport, Connecticut. He had really gotten carried away with the whole idea of being in this sort of company, and he was standing with his glass of champagne.

He stuck out his hand and said, "I'm Alfredo Dortenzio," but he yanked Mr. Frank's hand so ferociously, it shook his glass. The champagne went all over the place, and young Al said to Mr. Frank, "Don't just stand there! Get a sponge for the champagne."

Mr. Frank appeared shocked, and was probably wondering who in the world this kid thought he was. Mr. Truex was also a bit bent out of shape, but nothing ever came of it.

Later that day, we went to one of the great houses in Paris which Mr. Truex wanted us to see. I don't remember the owner's name, but he was supposedly a very famous Frenchman, and he also had an incredible house in Italy. In the afternoon, we had tea at his house in Paris. Of course, the butler opened the door wearing white gloves and cutaway tails, so we were all impressed. We, however, stood there in sneakers, blue jeans and T-shirts, and I thought Mr. Truex was going to drop dead from shock. No one had bothered to educate us on the proper outfits for visits to the upper crust. The next morning, we received a lecture on how to dress when you go to someone's house for tea. It was quite an experience.

In November of 1954, I arrived back in New York City from England after my time studying in Europe, again on the Ile De France. It was a rough trip across the Atlantic, but I don't get seasick, so I was in the dining room for every meal. When I was in Europe, I was nearly out of money, and therefore not eating much. Because of this, while I was on board, I ate like I had not been fed for days. The galley staff stared at me like I was some animal, and I am sure that I was quite a sight.

One day the purser called me to his office to discuss a problem with my luggage. I charged in without a serious thought in my head.

"We don't penalize passengers for luggage," he said, "unless it appears that someone is using a pleasure voyage to haul freight. One of your boxes weighs three hundred pounds, so you must tell me what it contains."

I answered with the first thing that came to mind, "It's a suit of armor."

He realized I was pulling his leg, but liked the way I pulled it. "You have a great mind," he said. "The penalty should be greater, but I'll reduce it to fifty dollars because of your clever answer."

In reality, the box actually contained lead urns I found to be stylistically irresistible, but if I had told him, I would have had a much heftier surtax to pay.

When I returned to New York from Europe, I had five trunks full of things, and thought I had done a great job of packing them. When the customs agent asked me what I had in each particular trunk, I just looked at my list and told him. Then, he would open the trunk and there would be something else there. I had all the lists mixed up, but, thankfully, he was amused.

When I finally got clear of customs, I had to get a truck to carry me to my apartment. When I left for Europe, I told my friend Larry Robinson that if he would rent an apartment that was cheap, I would share the rent. That way, when I got home, I would have a place to stay. I thought it was a great little apartment, but it was on the fifth floor, and a walk up. It was good for kids, but not so good for getting those damned trunks up there. When my mother came to see the apartment, she looked around and said that she really wanted to get a good look, because she was never coming back to climb those five flights again. Early the next year, Bill Leonard and I decided to get an apartment of our own that would suit us better.

Now I had to return to the real world, get a job, and go to work. It was about then that I understood what the teacher meant when he had said "When you finish school, you are just on the first step of the ladder, and you have to work your way up." I must have been on the right rung though, as I was offered a job at Lord and Taylor as a professional interior designer for thirty-five dollars a week.

When I was young, I didn't think much about the future. I was just "in the moment" when my career was beginning, and always wondering just how much money I would need to live like I wanted to in New York. Well, that is just the way I thought when Kandell, a Fabric House, offered me a job at almost double the pay I was making at Lord and Taylor. I don't remember doing any research on Kandell or even asking any questions. I just accepted their financial terms and decided to think about the details later. I knew I would rather work on 29th Street and have money than starve on the Upper East Side, and pretend I was being grand.

After all, I had worked at McCreery's to supplement my budget while studying at Parsons School of Design. Now, it seemed I had a chance to earn enough money to buy some luxuries and take some nice trips. When I jumped into the job at Kandell, I did not realize it would put me in a industry that related only indirectly to interiors, but, what the hell, I wanted the money.

As it turned out, going to work for Kandell was a real

artistic beginning for me. It put me into an industry that gave me a chance to use and grow my design skills. For the next thirty-six years, I worked in the curtain, drapery, linen and domestics lines. The job at Kandell led to subsequent positions with Bloomcraft, Bates, and Croscill. The money was great, but I think the recognition meant even more to me.

Making sixty dollars a week was not what I called a great beginning, but then I just had to think about the job at Lord and Taylor, and it seemed great. Kandell was a very Jewish firm, and when I told my family that I had gotten this job, they were very concerned that my employers would take advantage of a young Baptist Southern boy. That showed what little my family knew about me. I fit in fine at the company, liked everyone, and they seem to like the way I was willing to work hard and wanted to get ahead. Whatever they asked me to do, I did, figuring that at some point, they would realize I was a damn good catch.

Jerome Kandell was the owner and the boss. He was only about 5'4" tall and nearly that big around. He sounded really mean, but in truth, he was a great man to me. We got along well from the first day that I went to work there.

I called him "Mr. Jerome," instead of Mr. Kandell. It just seemed to match our business relationship. Since his brother was also employed by the firm, this also made it easier to separate the two in conversation. I worked there from about November 1954 until, 1960 or 1961. I don't remember the exact dates, but I do know that I learned quite a lot there.

Every evening, all the officers would line up at the door to say good night to Mr. Jerome. One evening, I jumped in at the end of the line and said, "Are you on your way home? Is your chauffeur waiting?"

"Yes," he said.

I answered, "Well, you go right past my apartment. Could just drop me off?"

He looked a little surprised, but said, "Get your coat and come on."

Man, at that point, all the big wheels stood there in shock. I just smiled and said, "See you guys tomorrow."

After I had been there about seven or eight months, he called at me, saying, "Boy! Come here."

I though the very least he could do was to learn my name, so I walked right into his office and told him, "My name is Randolph Trull, and everyone else here calls me Randy. It's all right if you call me Randy, too."

He looked a little taken back, but just said, "OK."

At work, things were still going well. Gabby, from Budapest, Hungary, was Jerome Kandell's second wife, and was only thirty-four. She spoke four or five different languages, and was absolutely gorgeous. She had dyed her hair red, and reminded me a little bit of Zsa Zsa Gabor, but she was very glamorous.

Mr. Kandell had a duplex apartment on the 32nd and 33rd floors at the Hampshire House in New York, a very fashionable and expensive address on Central Park. Gabby wanted the apartment to be redone to her liking, and since Kandell had told her I was an interior designer, she came to me to do the work. Mr. T.H. Robjohn-Gibbings had originally designed the apartment, and it had been done in a superb, contemporary style. At this point, I was only twenty-four years old, and a bit dumb about the real world.

When I arrived there, she came slinking down this grand staircase in a nothing more than a negligee. She told me, "Just call me Gabby."

I thought to myself, man I will lose this job in a heartbeat if that man thinks I am up here carrying on with his wife. I looked at her and said, "Well, I think I will call you Mrs. Kandell."

She started to tell me what things she wanted me to do in the apartment. One of the first things she said was that she wanted to have it repainted. It didn't look like it needed repainting, but if that was going to make her happy, I was going to keep her happy.

I arranged to have the painters come up there, and they gave her an outrageous price, just to repaint it in the same colors. The living room was white, but with a little touch of yellow in the paint so it came out a little bit creamy, just hinting towards yellow. The first time I got up there, after the painters had done their initial work, she took a pencil and marked all these bumps that she saw in the wall. She wanted them to take off these bumps, but when you put pencil marks on the wall, it was like a horror story to get them off.

I looked at the painter and said, "This looks like a nightmare of a job. I don't think you are going to be able to make any money on this."

He said, "Don't worry. I charged so much the first time that I will come out fine."

They finally did get the living room prepared to paint, but then she called me and said, "You have to come, Darling, and choose the color."

I went up there, and they had what must have been two hundred six-inch squares of white with a drop of yellow on the wall.

She said to me, "Which color?"

I could hardly tell the difference, so I just pointed to one and said, "That's the color!"

She said, "Perfect. Perfect!"

I went there a couple of days later, and she was screaming and carrying on. "The wall on the left doesn't match the wall on the right!" she exclaimed.

We tried to explain to her that the walls would never look the same in all conditions, due to lighting, but there was no pleasing her. We ended up painting nearly every wall a different color to finally get her happy. That was a tough job.

I walked into Mr. Jerome's office one evening, and he was sitting there with a customer. I said something like, "Could I wait a while and get a lift home, or I could borrow some money to take the subway?"

He just laughed and reached into his pocket, then handed me a fifty dollar bill. He said. "Do you think you can get change for that for the subway?"

I just looked at him and said, "No, but I have enough change in my pocket for the subway." Then he just looked at the customer, laughed and said, "What can I do with him? He is always one step ahead!" After this, he said, "Good night," and I got out of there.

As for the work I did there, I designed his showroom displays. One time I did one with a fabulous bird cage in it, and put real birds in the cage. It looked just great, but the birds would swing on the little swings and their guano would fly all over the place. It also stunk pretty badly unless cleaned every day. He bluntly told me to get rid of those damn birds, and to put stuffed ones in the cage.

A few days after that, he was working in the back office, and he sent for me to come over. Judy Morton, the head of the design department, had told him I was a designer. He had some fabrics pinned up on the wall, and he asked me what I thought about them. I told him what was wrong with them, and what needed to be done to make them saleable.

Everyone in the room looked a little surprised, but Mr. Kandell just said, "OK. That will be all," and I left the room. A few minutes later, he sent for me again, and told me that the company had hired a very famous interior designer to create this particular collection of coordinated fabrics, and that he wanted me to work with him. He said that the designer was T. H. Robsjohn-Gibbons, and that I was to go to his office.

What a thrill this was for me, as I knew who he was, and thought it was a lucky break to get a chance to work with such a great designer. Arriving at his office, I was a little nervous, but was sure that I could do the job asked of me. Actually, I may have even been a little cocksure that I would be able to do it.

He was very nice to me, and asked me what my name was. I said "Randolph Holland Trull."

He responded, "Write it down on a piece of paper," which I did. He then took a pencil, drew through some of the letters, and said "There. Now call yourself R. Holland Trull. That sounds very important, and people will remember it."

I dashed from his office to Tiffany's and ordered cards printed that way, then changed my signature at the bank to read that way, and thought, "Man, I have arrived." It sounded good, but no one ever knew who R. Holland Trull was. They all knew me as "Randy." Even today, everyone calls me Randy, but I still sign my checks R. Holland Trull.

We did get to work on the fabric collection, and it was a success. Mr. Kandell then asked me to design a line of fabrics for Kandell, and that surely was the beginning of my life in the "rag trade," as it is known to insiders. It seemed that whatever I did there worked. They made a lot of money, and Mr. Kandell was really good to me. Certainly, Mr. Kandell launched my career in the textile business. As for myself, I knew what I liked doing, but the problem was that I was still an interior designer at heart, and stayed involved there. It turned out to be a good blend of my own inner voice and his channeling me into the fabric business, since I was able to build a business by doing homes and apartments on the side my entire working life.

Oftentimes, people wonder where design ideas come from. With me, it has always been what is going on the marketplace, plus what I see that turns me on at the moment. During my time at Kandell, I noticed that designers were buying up lots of silks from Thailand. I figured if I could come up with a reasonably priced fabric that had the look of silk, we might just have a winner. Well, I took a shiny rayon yarn, wove a plaid, stripe, and solid together. The luster of the yarn made it look a little like silk and I did it in great colors all tied together in a coordinated program. I called it the "Siam Collection," and it turned out to be a winner. It really started my Kandell career off with a bang.

Mr. Kandell seemed delighted with me, and although he never gave me a bonus, he sent me to Europe for six weeks every year for six years, all expenses paid. I spent most of my time in the south of France, especially since it was beautiful and nearly all the designers came to Cannes. I met all of the well-known names in couture at this time, but few people outside of this sort of exclusive world had ever heard of them then.

As for my family, well, they did come visit me some. Early

on, I told Mr. Kandell they were coming to the city and he told me to bring them to his apartment. When we arrived, Mrs. Kandell was charming, and he was so great to my mother that she fell for him. She later told me how lucky I was to be working for someone so nice. Unfortunately, I never told him how his graciousness knocked down barriers that should not have been there. Let's face facts though: My parents just did not know his world, or anything about the Jewish faith.

Bill Leonard and I took an apartment together on Third Avenue, which, in late 1954, was not what you'd call the jewel of the century, but what we did with it made it one. It was what you'd call a "cold-water flat," which meant that it had no heat, but had hot water. It was on the second floor of a building between 61st and 66nd Streets, right in the middle of the block, so our back windows looked out on the beautiful gardens of all the rich people living on that street. We paid $125 a month, and I told Billy that it was too much, so I went to the rent board and asked for a reduction. After a year, they came to see it, said I was right, and reduced it to seventy-five dollars a month. They also made it retroactive to the time we moved in, but the landlord appealed the decision, this time so they came out and looked again. Then they reduced it to fifty-five dollars a month, and made him pay the difference, dating from the time of our move-in date. What a deal we got from a little persistence there!

When Billy eventually got married, I rented one of the rooms for seventy-five dollars a month, so I was clearing twenty bucks a month profit. One evening we had a grand party, but you must remember this was a building from the outside that looked like it was going to fall down. People were a little shocked when they arrived, but when they came inside they loved it. Hermione Gingold, who was well-known for her role in Gigi, arrived in a full-length mink coat.

When I asked her if I could take her coat, she looked at me and said, "No thank you, as I understand that this is a cold-water flat." But believe me, we had plenty of heat. Remember that my father was in the heating business, and he had solved that problem. Maybe she thought I just wanted the coat, and she was not terribly wrong: I would have looked great in it.

The apartment I rented on Third Avenue was really unusual since we lived on the second floor, but the third and fifth floors were empty, so we had the uppermost level, and no neighbors above. It got photographed dozens of times by magazines and catalogue photographers looking for particular settings. It ended up being published in the oddest places, but really served me well as a palette. When one of the magazines called to ask if I had a room they could take pictures of, I would just redo one of the rooms, or a particular section, of the apartment. It was like a movie set, ever-changing to fit the storyline needed.

Bill Leonard, Paul Sessa, and I decided to open up a shop on East 66th Street, but could not decide what to call it. I came up with a name that, little did I know, would become well-known. I took the letters "TR" from Trull, "ESS" from Sessa and "ARD" from Leonard, and Tressard was born. I knew nothing about French, but I said let's put an accent over the "E," and it will sound French. It was to be an antiques shop, except that it turned out I was still doing fabrics for Kandell, so it became more than that.

By this time, I thought I knew everything you can know about fabric, so I designed a line for a division of Kandell that he owned on the West Coast. When the president of that division arrived in New York to see his new line, I showed him what I thought was the last word in fabric. Without telling anyone I went to Burlington, bought three thousand yards of mattress ticking, and had it printed. When I showed the president what I had created for him, he said something like "I would never put that crap in my line." It went through my mind that this was going to be the end of my job when they found out I had printed all that fabric. To prevent that, I bought it all and announced to the boys at Tressard that we were going into the fabric business, and that the designers would love this stuff. I think they thought I had lost my mind, but I told them, "Have no fear—I will figure out how to get this stuff on the market."

I was one of the charter members of the National Society of Interior Designers (NSID), which was formed in the city since we did not want to be called "decorators," but preferred "designers" instead. I was the national program director, so I came up with the idea to show home furniture fabrics in ready-to-wear designs at a luncheon, and each fabric company would show their fabric in ready-to-wear as well. As friend Ethel Merman was so famous for saying, "You have got to have a gimmick," so I went down to 12th St. and Second Avenue, stood at the stage door, and when a not-so-well-known star came out, I asked her if she would model mattress ticking for me in a fashion show. She said yes, but only if I would not tell anyone her true measurements. When I introduced her at the lunch, it went something like this: "Introducing Miss Once-Upon-A-Mattress, Carol Burnett, wearing mattress ticking from Tressard."

With that, we were launched, sold thousands of yards, and told everyone it would fade and shrink, but what a look for them, and what a profit for us.

Carol and I had dinner a number of times, and I did try to help her do the interior of her first apartment on 56th Street. I am not sure it was really her first apartment, but it was the one she had just rented then, so to me, it was the first. One evening, we were going out to dinner and I came to get her in my new 1959 Buick Skylark convertible. Carol had on a new mink stole and looked great. As we pulled up by the theater, we saw her fellow actors from *Once Upon A Mattress* carrying their protest signs since they were on strike (or involved in a "lock-out" dispute, as it was called).

One of the girls said to Carol, "Having it rough, aren't you?" With that, Carol threw the mink back into the car, picked up a sign, and started marching. She then told me to pick her up at the corner in twenty minutes. After that, we went on to dinner.

Soon after this, Carol asked me if I knew of any apartments for rent, and one morning we went up to 53rd Street to look at a penthouse that I told her was available. This was being rented by Carol Lawrence, notable for her role in *West Side Story* and her marriage to Robert Goulet. Lo and behold, Carol's mother was in town visiting, and she invited us to have breakfast with them.

I knew nothing about the theatre, and when something was said about *West Side Story*, I just turned to Carol Lawrence and said, "I see it is coming back to Broadway. Will you be doing it again?"

She looked at me like I was the devil, and said "No."

Boy did I feel really dumb, until a few days later. It was then I read in the paper that she would be doing the show again. After I saw this, I called Carol Burnett, and she just laughed at me and said, "Fellow, you don't know the theatre."

What a great lady, and a jewel of a person she is. Just two years ago, when she did a show on Broadway, I made an investment in it, just to say, "Thanks from an old man that you helped get started."

I have always said that mother was a strong lady, but it was proven even more when she had breast cancer. She had a breast removed, but she did not want anyone to know it, so when she went to have the chemotherapy treatment, she would park her car around the comer so no one would know she was there. After the treatments, she would go to a lunch meeting even though she would tell me she felt like hell, just to keep up appearances.

I came home to try and cheer her up, but that was not really necessary as this was a lady that dealt with things really well. As soon as she felt up to traveling, we drove to New York. I did my homework, and found that she could have a matching breast made so she could better fit into her clothes. I took her to the shop where they weighed the breast she had, and made her one to match in size and weight. She could wear that one since they looked the same, and it would not affect her shoulder posture since it allowed her balance. It was a great uplifting thing for her spirit, and she went home not feeling half, but whole again. What a lady, and what strength she possessed.

I thought things were fine, and that was the end of all of the fear that I had, but little did I know that there was more to come. A year later, in 1960, they put her back into the hospital and took out one of her lungs, and that was when I realized that things were not good. She never let it show, and had a strong will that served her well. She flew through all this with flying colors, and made us all think things were great. She seemed like her old self, and things seemed to settle back into a normal pace. We all had the feeling she was going to be fine, but we were very wrong.

The '50s ended with worries about Mother's health, but a new warmer feeling for Dad. Often, I would fly home for a weekend just to see my family. I would sit around a lot talking with Mother and Dad, then, at some point, I would drive over to Franklin Street to pick up Grandmother and Granddaddy and take them out to eat. That was my routine and most of my trips back to Raleigh were very uneventful. I was lulled into thinking that home help no surprises for me, but, boy, was I wrong.

I got up one Saturday morning and my father said, "What are you going to do today?"

I stood there in shock. I thought, "Why is he asking me this?" He had never asked me that in the twenty-eight years I had been around. I looked at him and told him I planned to go downtown and see if I could find any of my old friends. To my even greater surprise, he said he wanted to go with me.

I thought, "What has happened to my father?" So, the two of us headed off to downtown Raleigh and I remembered I needed to get some film developed. He told me to stop at Mr. Daniels' shop since he was one of Dad's old buddies.

When we walked into the store, everyone said, "Hello, Monk." Well, what do you know?

He turned to them and said, "Hello, this is my son Ran. the *News and Observer* ran an article about him yesterday."

I stood there with tears rolling down my eyes. I could hardly believe I was hearing him say that. Finally, he was proud of me.

Above: The "Blue Room" and "Red Room" in Randy's Third Avenue apartment both made appeareance in *House and Garden* magazine, in the
late 1950s. Below Left: Randy created the window effect using 16,000
lucite beads. Below Right: By the time *House and Garden* magazine ran
this photo of Randy's New York apartment, he was busy redecorating, in
hopes of catching a new wave of publicity.

5 | *After School:*
Going Wild in the Sixties

BY 1960, I FELT LIKE a real New Yorker. I had truly made it my home. I even found a church home there, too. First I visited a Baptist church in Manhattan, but I did not like it at all. It was not the kind of Baptist church I was used to. Then, I visited Central Presbyterian Church, on Park Avenue and 64th Street. I felt right at home there and was elected to the board of deacons not long after I joined the church.

No matter how busy my life became, I always made time for Edith Hood. She felt that she had no one else in the world, so she treated me as though I was her son. After her husband's death, she called me often, and I later invited her to visit me in New York City. She had no money, so I took care of all her expenses, and made sure that she had enough clothes. This was back when social security was next to nothing. If I remember correctly, she got something like fifty-two dollars a month, but certainly not enough live off of, or even to eat. It just seemed the right thing to do to take care of her those last few years of her life.

At one point, she lived alone in Atlantic City, and got very sick. Her neighbors called to tell me that she was in the hospital, and told me that I would have to come down to give my permission for an operation she needed. Evidently, she had told them that I was her child and that I had the right to approve or disapprove of anything. I gave them permission to operate while on the telephone, and then drove to Atlantic City right in the middle of the week. When I got there, everyone talked to me very openly since they thought I was family. I never corrected them, because I realized that she felt so alone. I left Atlantic City on Thursday, after I saw that the operation had gone fine.

I returned to New York because I was working, and I needed to get back to my job. I told Mrs. Hood that I

When Mabel and Monk Trull flew to Europe in 1962, Mrs. Trull made the New York runway a fashion runway in her Jackie Kennedy-style ensemble. Randy's two nieces joined in the fashion statement. (Eastern Air Lines)

would be back on Saturday. On Friday evening, the hospital called and told me that she had gone to sleep and did not wake up. I was shocked, and had to think about where and how I would arrange the funeral. I was the only person she felt close to, and she had told me what she wanted to happen. She wanted to be buried beside her husband, out in Brooklyn, but I've forgotten the name of the cemetery now. It's sort of amusing, but in this particular cemetery, they actually bury the bodies three-people deep since space is at a premium. Mr. Hood's first wife was already buried there, and he was buried on top of her. The Mrs. Hood I had known was going to be buried on top of him, making it a Mr. Hood sandwich!

I had to notify the cemetery to prepare, and had to look around for a funeral home. The one I found was very nice, and I told them that there didn't have to be any reception service because there wasn't anybody but me. They said that they could send a hearse down to get the body in Atlantic City. I told them that I would like to have the funeral on Monday, but they said that they couldn't do that because the gravediggers were all booked up. "The only time that we could get her into the ground this week is if you can have her out at the cemetery by ten o'clock on Tuesday morning," they said. New York City is a weird place to try to get things done, so I said, "Fine, if that is the only time to get her into the ground, then it's Tuesday at ten o'clock."

I went to Atlantic City to sign all of the papers. For some reason, everyone in the office was very nice to me. They said, "We are sorry about your loss, you have our deepest sympathies. How would you like to pay for her bill?"

"Bill?" I said.

"Yes," they replied, "before you can take the body you owe us six hundred dollars."

I said, "I don't have that kind of money, and neither does she!" For a kid working in New York in 1963, six or seven hundred dollars was a lot of money.

I just sat there and explained to them that I was not kin to her, that I was just a friend. They replied, "Well, you can't take the body if you don't pay us the money."

I pointed at them, then at the body, and said, "If I understand you correctly, you are saying that you are not going to release the body to me for the burial, unless, I pay you the six hundred dollar hospital bill." They said, "That's right!"

"Oh, OK," I said, "there is no one else in the world that is going to be at that funeral except me. I'm not giving you the money and you can keep the body. I'll go in the chapel and say my prayers, and then I'll go on home."

All of the blood drained from the man's face as he stammered, "But, but you can't do that!"

"Oh yes I can!" I said. Because you told me that I have two choices, either pay you, or I can't take the body! Keep the body! But the six hundred dollars you are never going to see from me. You can put a lien on everything in the world that she owns. If you can find the six hundred dollars, please be my guest."

They had a little conference and decided that they couldn't keep her. They would much rather be stuck with her bill than be stuck with her body. One of the girls in the room interrupted our argument and chimed in, "Mr. Trull, you need to calm down. You are overreacting about this whole situation. Somebody get a wine glass for him so I can pour him a drink."

As they stumbled over each other to get a glass for me, an older gentleman in back replied, "I'm sorry sir, but all of our wine glasses are clear." I couldn't believe what I was hearing. Whoever heard of having to drink out of a red wine glass!

I called the different people that I knew who were kin to Mr. Hood, but found none that were claimed kin to Mrs. Hood because she was his third wife. All of his relatives were just distant relations. I let them know that I was holding this little service on Tuesday morning. Then I made the decision to try and track down her family, whom I knew she hadn't spoken to in over twenty-eight years. I knew she was from Pittsburgh, and I knew what her maiden name was, so I called information in Pittsburgh and asked for McCullough. They said that there were two of them listed, a junior and a senior. I knew that her brother had had one child. Ms. Hood had told me to write her family a letter after her death, just to tell them that she had died.

I decided to call these folks instead, and I got the younger McCullough on the phone. I told him who I was and what I was calling about, and he said that she was his only aunt. I told him that I was having a service, and that I thought that he should at least know that she had passed away, and where she would be buried. He was a very nice young man. On the other hand, the people from Mr. Hood's side of the family, which were no kin to her at all, gave me a hard time over everything.

Anyway, on the morning of the would-be graveside service, I had a limousine pick me up, and had a female friend to go with the preacher and me from my church. I asked him to just say a prayer, out at the cemetery. When we drove down to the funeral home, I said that I would like to see her once more. I just wanted to know in my mind that it was Edith who had passed away, and the funeral directors were very nice.

They ushered me into a little office, told me how sorry they were, and gave me the bill, which meant that I had to pay the bill before I could see the body. I had gotten out of paying the hospital bill, but I had always planned to pay her funeral costs. I wrote the check, then we walked into the chapel where there were maybe four or five people sitting around, but I didn't know who they were. I walked up in the front and looked at Edith Hood. There were three or four flower arrangements, and I took the cards off them to see whom they were from, then stood there for a few minutes and said a prayer.

As I walked out into the foyer of the chapel, some man walked up to me, and cussed me out. I'm standing with my preacher on one side, and this gal friend of mine on the other, and he lets loose. I looked at him and said," Who are you?"

He said that he was Mr. Hood's third cousin, which made him absolutely no kin to Edith at all.

"I'm sorry that you waited to come see her until she was dead," I told him. "It would have been nice if you had come to see her when she was alive." I turned to another young couple that was standing there and said, "I'm sorry, I don't know anybody here. Who are you?" The man said they were Mr. and Mrs. McCullough, although I can't remember their first names. He said that he and his wife had driven all this way from Pittsburgh just for the funeral, and I thought that it was very nice.

When we got back in the limousine and headed to the cemetery, I asked the director of the funeral home, "Exactly why had this man cussed me out?" It was a weird thing, but they had a custom in this funeral home that the last person to see the deceased was the family. Since I was paying the bill, they presumed that I was the family. They asked everyone else to step out of the chapel while I was alone with Edith. It was sort of ironic that the only person who was real family blood was asked to leave the room, and he thought that he had been deliberately excluded from the service.

It's rather sad when you think about it: Someone's life

had come to an end. There were so few people who were concerned about her, but everyone was concerned about her "things." The only people who didn't seem interested in material possessions were her few distant family members. After the burial, I invited the McCullough's to come back to my house for lunch.

When we got back to the house, I said that I had found a pocket watch in her belongings. It was a very beautiful gold watch, and I told Mr. McCullough that, based on the engravings, I thought it had belonged to his grandfather. I told him that this should be something that stays with the family. I also gave him several other personal things that I had found that I thought belonged to the family, and he was very appreciative. That was one of those moments in life when you realize that all of our lives are going to come to an end, but you're just not sure when it will happen.

1962 was the year in my life when all things came crashing down, one brick after another. There were times when I wondered if I was strong enough to withstand it all. To explain this better, I should go back to my Parsons school days for a minute to let you know about a girl named Abby Munroe.

It is hard to remember just when I got all tied up with Abby. We had been good friends at Parsons, but she was engaged to someone else, and the thought of us as a couple never occurred to me until after I returned from Europe. I gave her a call and asked her if she wanted to go out. She accepted and, from that night on, our feelings grew. It became apparent that this was no passing friendship.

Abby was tall and had wonderful eyes and a great smile. We laughed a lot at nothing kinds of things. Since we both were interior designers, we had a lot of common ground. She was working as an interior decorator at Thedlow Company at the time. Our bonds became stronger after a few months and we began to talk about getting married. Of course, that meant it was time for our families to meet.

Abby and her brother, Tim, were adopted. Their adoptive father, Dr. Bela Mittelmann, died in 1959. He was a renowned psychiatrist and psychoanalyst. Abby's mother, Ruth, and her second husband invited my parents and me for dinner one night and things went well with the older generation. Our parents got along fine, but Abby's stepfather, Dr. Parkes, always seemed intimidating to me. Like her adopted father, he was a renowned psychiatrist and one of the most intelligent people I have ever known. I hardly knew what to say around him, so Abby and I just sat there and smiled at each other that night.

Randy's fiancé, Abby Monroe, is pictured here at Cape Cod, in 1961. "It's a fabulous picture," said Randy. "She was darling. She grew up on the Cape and had a lot of fun in her."

Abby didn't want an engagement ring. She just wanted a wedding band with baguettes all the way around it, so instead of an engagement ring, I bought her a bracelet from Bugatti and had it turned into a watch. Today, you can find that sort of thing all over the place, but then you had to have it custom made.

Abby had her own apartment, at 239 Central Park West, and I would stay there sometimes. Bill Leonard and I were roommates, so Abby and I seldom had any privacy at my place. Bill had been dating his girlfriend, Betty, for some time, and the four of us went out together a lot. Bill and Betty would be married in 1962.

Back in the fall of 1961, Abby and I were supposed to go to a football game in Philadelphia, but Abby's feet swelled up, and she could not put her shoes on.

This photo of Randy and Abby was taken at the Waldorf-Astoria, about 1959.

At the time, we did not think much about it. A few weeks later, her leg became badly swollen. When I spoke to my mother on the phone, I said to her that it was strange that different parts of her body were having this swelling problem. I blurted out it might be something like leukemia, moving around. My mother lit into me about that, and said that it was a terrible thing to think. To tell you the truth, I never thought about it again for months, because Mother really put that out of my mind. All that came to a halt in January, 1962 when Abby was hospitalized.

I told Abby's mother that I did not think she would need a private room since she was just going into the hospital for a check-up. Her mother said that some of the tests would be rough, and she wanted her to have a private room. I should have gotten the message without having things spelled out so clearly to me, but I did not. I should have both listened and heard what she was saying, especially since she was a doctor.

Abby went into the hospital just before Christmas, so I had a Christmas tree made out of gum drops for her room. When I visited her there, she seemed fine. I would make her a martini, her favorite drink, and we would laugh and chat like nothing in the world was really wrong. She spoke to my mother on the phone, and told her that as soon as she got out she would visit her in Raleigh for a few days.

Suddenly, on a Wednesday, Abby's condition was listed as critical. Her mother said that she had an infection in her intestines and that it would take a few days for it to clear up. She told me things would be fine in about a week. On Sunday, I sat with her while she had her martini, and I told her I would be back up on Monday afternoon.

I worked for myself then, and I could spend lots of time with her. On Monday morning, I had some plans for a job that I needed to photocopy, and worked on that. It was just past three when I called the hospital to tell Abby that I would be a little late. The nurse answered the phone, and told me to call Abby's mother before I came to the hospital.

I knew then that things could not be good, so I called Ruth. She asked me to come to her apartment before I went to the hospital, as she wanted to talk with me.

I dashed up to her apartment on Central Park West, and we sat in the living room. She said that Abby had had leukemia, and that she died just before three that afternoon. I was in such a state of shock that I really don't know what in the world I was thinking, but she just kept talking. Ruth also told me that she knew this was going to happen, and that she made the decision not to tell anyone, not even Abby's brother, as she did not want Abby or anyone else to know that there was no hope.

She told me that she was going to have Abby cremated, and asked me if I had a problem with that. I think I said "She is your daughter, and that is your decision," but I really don't remember. She went on to say the cremation would be the next day, that there would then be a service on Wednesday, and then she gave me a hug.

I left the apartment, not sure what to do or where to go, and just stood out on the street crying, attempting to put my thoughts together. I got into a cab and went back to my apartment and started making calls. Within what seemed like minutes, my apartment was full of friends, and we all just sat around trying to make some sense of what had happened. I called my parents, and later that evening, two dozen roses arrived at my apartment from my grandmother. The next day, my apartment looked like a flower shop.

My mother called and asked if I wanted her to come to New York, but I said, "No," as Abby was already gone, and there was really nothing that could be done at this point. The date was January 8, 1962, and that date has more meaning in my life than nearly any other. I thought about the way her mother handled it, and it really bothered me. Now I realize that Ruth made it easy for me. I never saw her body and I try not to think of Abby as dead. I just think of her as someone who has gone away. I have beautiful thoughts of Abby, wonderful memories, even today, as though she might just walk right into this room. If she did, I imagine she would still be the same beautiful person I thought would fill my life.

Life does not end as we all seem to think it will, but we go on, trying to think what is ahead of us, not what has just passed. As for me, I think that what my mother said just after Abby's death was a great thing, and it did make me think more about what my life seemed to be all about. She said, "Son, there are things that happen in life that we all would like to change, but try to deal with it this way. Your life is so full and you are so busy, that maybe marriage and a family are not the things you will need most. Your brother needs a wife and children, and that makes his life full, but you are so busy going and doing, that this just may not be what makes your life full." I am not sure that she really felt that way, but maybe she was trying to say that life does not give you everything you want, so take what it has to offer and make the best of it.

About this time, I did some freelance work for Heritage Furniture and Collins & Aikman, working for each about three months. Between these and some savings, I managed to buy my first house in the Hamptons, and begin what would turn out to be a profitable side life in real estate.

I was truly busy as I could be, and what went on that spring seems hard to remember. Betty and Billy had a house on Fire Island, and they invited me out all the time, so spring seemed full of work, weekends at the beach, and planning a trip around the world to work on some new ideas that I had for the textile business. Offers to work for other firms came to me, as I had finally made a real name for myself, but I ignored them, and worked hard at Bates. Little did I know that they would fire me in late 1969.

My parents were going off to Monte Carlo for a Shriners' International convention, and we made plans to meet in Madrid, at the Hilton, in early June. Since I planned to head around the world after that, it worked well for me. Earlier, I said

Bill and Betty Leonard eye the birdcage in their New York apartment warily, about 1961.

that had not been the best year, and things did not change.

Betty got sick, and the doctors said that she had pneumonia. It did not seem to be a big deal at first, but suddenly she got worse and went into the hospital. Ironically, it was the same hospital that Abby had been in, and Betty was even on the same floor. She'd had asthma for many years, so the pneumonia she had developed made things very difficult for her.

Monday, June 7th was one really bad day, and I had an awful fight with a friend. I went home to cool off, then spoke to Billy. He had checked on Betty, and told me she had an emergency tracheotomy that morning, but that she was fine now. He told me not to come that evening because she was sleeping, and that I should wait until the next day.

This seemed to make sense, so I went home, and got to bed about ten. The phone rang about thirty minutes after I had dropped off to sleep, and it was Billy. He was crying, and said that Betty was probably dying.

I rolled out of bed, threw on some clothes, and dashed across the street to the garage where I kept my car. My parents' car was in the same garage as mine, since they had left it there before going to Europe, and it was blocking mine. I jumped into it, and came out of the garage flying like a bat out hell, but turned too short, and mashed in the passenger side door on their car.

I didn't care. At that point, all I could think of was getting to the hospital and seeing Betty.

When I got to the room, a friend of Billy's was crying, and his friend David was there with him. In between sobs of anguish, Billy told me that Betty had gone into a coma. The doctors felt that she would not recover as she had been that way too long. They were concerned that if she came out of the coma, she would already have enough brain damage that she would never be the same. I do not remember much clearly after that news, but I did talk with the doctors, and it did not seem she was going to make it. The room was filled with machines that were keeping her alive, and it all seemed hopeless.

A little after midnight, they said that she was gone, and I went into her room and had the nurses take her off all the machines. After they left, I brushed her hair, put on her makeup, and made her look better. I really did not want Billy to see her as she had looked the moment of her death, but I knew he would not leave until he saw her. What a nightmare week this had turned out to be.

We took Billy back to his apartment, and then started to call his family in Connecticut. Hers lived in New Hampshire, and they knew she was in bad shape, so they had already started heading to New York. Because of this, we couldn't tell them until they arrived that she had died, and that would be probably around two or three in the morning. Bill's mother and stepfather arrived, and I told them just to go to bed at my apartment, as I would be there with Bill so I could to wait for Betty's parents to arrive.

We had the funeral in New York City at the Campbell's Chapel. As the preacher spoke, he commented that he had never seen such a group of sharply-dressed people, or such beautiful flowers. Everyone was dressed superbly, and the personally-done arrangements each seemed to show that her friends were all very artistic, and that they had put their feelings into the work. After the funeral in New York, her family wanted to take her to New Hampshire for a funeral there. She died on Monday, and by the time we managed to get things arranged in New Hampshire for the second ceremony, it was Friday, and I thought Bill was going to fall apart. I wondered myself how I was going to make it, but it is in times like that you do find there is more strength inside than you realize. You don't really think about it, but it just comes out.

Abby's death on January 7th and then Betty's death on June 7th of that same year—on the same floor of the same hospital—made me do a hell of a lot of thinking. I am not sure whether there was some sort of message that I was supposed to get or not, but it surely made me wonder about life. With all this going on, I changed my departure ticket to Europe, and bought another one for Bill. I felt as though he needed some time to think about things and to put his life back together. Our first stop was Madrid, where I planned to see my family.

We arrived early in the morning, and I went straight to Mother and Dad's room to tell them the news. Dad was downstairs having breakfast, so I told mother the bad news, and that Bill was in the room here, too. She said that she knew something had happened, as she dreamed it, but did not know what it was—just something.

I went downstairs to the dining room to tell Dad, and he was sitting there alone, trying to talk to the waiter, who was looking at him like he was some kind of a nut. He was throwing his arms in the air, saying "chickens," quacking like a duck, saying "egg" and pantomiming flying around, while saying "scramble."

I asked, "What is the problem?"

"These damn foreigners don't understand," he said. "All I want is scrambled eggs." I tried to remind him that he was the foreigner, and that this was their country. At this point, he said they could have it: All he wanted was scrambled eggs. I think it is safe to say he was not much of a traveler.

When Bill and I left Madrid, we just wandered around Europe for a couple of weeks, then headed back home. For him, home was very different from what it had been before, and trying to think of the future, instead of living in the past, was no easy task. It would take him a long time to adjust to losing Betty.

For me, getting back to the office and trying to come up with new ideas was easy. Dealing with salesmen was a little more difficult, but I always seemed to come out on top. I just kept doing what I was used to doing, and expecting something great to happen. Then something occurred that truly amazed me. Bates decided to go into ready-to-wear men's wear, and they asked me if I would design a line of sportswear. Maybe they asked me because I dressed to-the-nines, no matter what day of the week it was, whether I had anywhere special to go after work or not. Maybe they just thought I was crazy enough to come up with something completely new that would sell. Either way, I was flattered to get the assignment.

Given that I've been a dresser sense I was a child, designing clothes was a real treat. I've always loved to shop and look like a fashion book, so I jumped at the assignment like some mad person. It proved to be a real challenge, though. I gave it my best even though I now know why so many people say that clothing designers are crazy. It pulls everything out of you. You are not dealing with just a window treatment or a bed covering. You are decorating the human body.

Our office became an even madder place, quickly. One hour, I would be an artist designing bedspread fabric. The next hour, I might be running around behind the file cabinets to try on clothes. How lucky I was to be the perfect model size then! All the samples fit me perfectly, and all I had to do was tell the tailor how to alter things so that the designs would be faithful to my drawing. So here I was going off again on another challenge and wondering where it might lead.

I did not analyze it then, but I look back now and see that I was cutting a fresh fashion path. It was not unheard of that ready-to-wear designers would switch to fashioning home furniture, but it was extremely rare for home furniture artists to suddenly draw up a line of clothing. I designed the clothes to have a Cossack look, and I used bold colors that previously had not been used in men's wear. Then I added the mix and match bonus of a fully coordinated wardrobe. At first, we called the line Sir Bates, but then the company changed that name to Bratten Original.

Once I finished designing the line, we told the company we wanted to have a breakfast-hour fashion event at the Four Seasons restaurant to show the media and customers the new line. I made sure it was up to me to decide which model would wear which clothes. The modeling agency sent dozens of young guys to my office, but I could only pick a handful to show off the line.

The other employees at Bates had a good time listening to me order the models around. Repeatedly, I made them walk up and down a "runway" we created from a slice of empty office space. I listened to the other employees opinions, but

Randy's Sir Bates line debuted at the 1967 Men's Wear Fashion Show in New York. Randy, Edward Lee Cave, Jack Rogers of W. R. Grace, Mabel Trull, Mrs. Armand Ginsberg (Chairman of the Board for Bate), Robert L. Green (*Playboy Magazine*), and Monk Trull sit at the runway.

made my own decisions about which models I would use based solely on my opinion. I watched each one walk the runway and then, sometimes, would think to myself, "Gosh, he looks great in those mad clothes I designed!"

Next, I gave them another test. I had choreographed the whole fashion show in my mind so that the models constantly were stripping off pieces of clothing then redressing to demonstrate the coordination of the fashion elements. So I made each one of them show me they could do this gracefully before I made my final choices.

The actual fashion show was a big ego blast for me, but it surely was a headache, too. I sat at the head of the table and acted like King or Queen—your choice. Mother and Dad were there to watch another of their son's mad ideas materialize. We had great coverage in

Randy brought his own interior-line fabrics, colors, and textures when he ventured into the men's fashion field. "Since I've never designed apparel before, I felt free," Randy told a reporter from the *News and Observer* in 1967.

the press and the line was successful for two seasons, but, soon, I was headed back to my love—designing home furniture. The frenzied, ultra-competitive world of ready-to-wear temporarily wore me out.

Above: Randy designed apparel of ease. His suede cloth bulky knit pull-over featured snap closures under the shoulder buttons.

Below: Randy designed a line of Cossack-style clothes in the mid-1960s that gained a lot of attention. "Trull is obviously at home at any drawing board," said Lynn Litwin of the *Daily News Record*.

"I chose all the models and they had to look good and be able to handle themselves well on the runway. I had them switching everything around out there to demonstrate just how interchangeable the clothes I designed were," said Randy, in 2009.

Randy designed this four-piece outfit from slipcover fabric by Charles Bloom.
Cold water laundering had just been developed and Colgate-Palmolive
sponsored the fashion show at the Four Seasons.

Randy Trull

I HEADED OFF SHORTLY AFTER that for a trip around the world with meetings planned in Spain, India Formosa, Hong Kong, South Korea, Japan and home. Madrid was my first stop and I stayed at the Constantia Hilton. I went out walking the first day there, and ran into Nella, a friend of mind from New York. She said we should go out on the town for the evening, and I agreed. I rushed back to the hotel to get dressed and found that I had packed two left shoes. I thought, what a nightmare, as the Spaniards didn't make shoes wide enough for my feet. I bought a pair that I could hardly wear, and went out for the evening.

I headed for India the next day, where I was invited by some of India's biggest manufacturers to be their guest. When I landed in Bombay, I felt like I was making one of those crazy movies with all sorts of strange people looking at me. Fans were running on the ceiling and the lights were very low. The car I took looked like something made in the '30s, and the driver rushed me to the Taj Mahal Hotel, which was really very nice. The only problem was that at this point, they did not know how to control the air conditioner so you had to make a choice to freeze or to cook. I chose to freeze as the odor outside was more than I could deal with, so I just piled all my clothes on the bed and slept under them to keep from catching cold. Everyone was really very warm and kind to me, and I must say that I really loved everyone. The Indians are truly warm people who did everything to make my trip super.

The first night there, an American couple was with me, and the man was good enough to tell me what to eat and to touch, and what to avoid. The next evening, I was on my own and was invited to one of India's leading furniture manufacturer's home for dinner. It was a high-rise apartment, simply beautiful, and the living room was at least thirty-five feet long. They had invited fifteen or twenty people to dinner, and it was set up as a buffet. With no one to help me choose what to eat, I tried to take what I thought would work. When I took my first bite, it burned my insides out. Suddenly, the hostess asked me how I liked the food, and I looked up to the sky and tried to respond, but nothing would come out of my mouth. I had either lost or burned my voice out! She realized this and turned to the butler and said, "I think he needs a glass of water." I thought a hose would be more like it.

They took me into a shop filled with tiger skins. It was so hot and smelled so badly that I thought I would pass out. As I was leaving Bombay to fly to Delhi, they gave me a large bouquet of flowers. I headed toward to the plane, thinking I was some glamorous star with an arm full of flowers. As I bounced up the steps of the French Caravelle airplane, I hit the 5'9" door about mid-forehead with my 6'1" height, and passed out. I never did let go of the flowers, so there I lay, like a fresh corpse, with flowers on my chest.

The attendants put cold rags on my head which revived me, threw out the flowers, and off we went to Delhi. When we arrived, two very nice young ladies from the government met me and drove me to a hotel, where I stayed for two days before they came back and informed me that they had taken me to the wrong hotel.

After I finally got to the right spot, I was invited to visit the Taj at Agra. They had arranged the trip by train, and when we arrived at the station, I went right to first class and sat down. I was then told I would have to change my seat, at which point I said, "I sit here or I don't go." There was much talk, none of which I understood, but I stayed right where I was, while the ladies sat in another car during the trip. They had arranged a first class bus ride to the Taj, and I think it would be safe to say that the bus was probably made in late 1920s. There was no air conditioning, and all the windows were open, so we got all the dust from the road and the hot air all at one time. It really made for a nightmare of a trip, but when I finally got there, it was all worthwhile.

Leaving India turned out to be another new experience for me, as they gave me more flowers, thanked me for visiting, and I headed into customs where they asked if I had any Indian money. I showed them what was about twenty-five dollars in Indian money, and they asked me where I got it. I told them that the nice ladies had changed my money, and from that point it went straight to hell. They said that it was not legal, and started going through my address book page by page, looking for something fishy to their eyes.

It was well over a hundred degrees in there, the flowers were beginning to smell too sweet, and I was getting a bit carried way with the whole scene. I then threw the flowers and a handful of magazines at the inspector, and told him to take the darn money. I just wanted to leave, and in the meantime, people were sitting out on the plane, cooking alive, waiting for me to board. Somehow the ladies stepped in and got everyone calm. As I boarded the plane, I thought what a joke about those flowers it turned out to be. They were intended as a sign of safe journey, yet they had nearly been my undoing.

Once I finally departed, I flew from Delhi to Hong Kong. I landed in the evening, and boy was it exciting! There were three thousand people there, throwing sticks and stones to protest the latest government actions. I do love a crowd, but was not involved with this one. The police there were very nice, and drove me to the hotel in a police car. The Hilton was just around the corner from the governor's house, so the Chinese protesters had encircled the whole block. In order to get out, you had to pass through them. As I was of the old belief that if you can't beat them, join them, I bought a picture of Mao and his little red book. When I came out of the hotel, I would hold the book up and say I am with you (at least until I got into the cab). The management put me on the 26th floor of the hotel, but I told them I would have to be moved down to a lower floor because I had found that I could not easily walk to the lobby from there. They had recently found a bomb in the elevator shaft, and I thought it was too far from the 26th floor to safety if I had to run.

While there, I met with lots of companies that wanted to do business with Bates, but the one that stands out in my mind was owned by a very nice Indian man named Bob Murjani. He was chairman of the Murjani Group and was famous in the design world. Bob invited me to his home, and what a house it was. It was like nothing I had ever seen. At that time, it was known as Hong Kong's most expensive residence, but I wish he had known to call me about the appointments. Some of the things he had in there made me remember a line that says nothing good, but is not unkind. Auntie Mame said it, so I decided to say it. "I just can't tell you what I think of this house!"

The pool was big enough to scuba dive in, and the dining room table was round with a disk in the middle that would drop down, so colored fountains could spray up in the middle. The faucets in the bathroom were all made out of ivory, with elephants all in a row. The chandelier in the dining room was all cut crystals, and swung out over a table that would seat twenty-four. It was made in Italy, where they had supposedly bought a mountain to get enough crystals to make the thing. Bob wanted me to go into business with him, but all I could think of was that it would be mad to go into business with this man. Just remember that I did not say anywhere in this book that I was very smart, just lucky, but this is not one of those lucky moments. I did not take him up on his offer, but Gloria Vanderbilt did, and I am told she made a fortune in blue jeans. Oh well, you can't win them all!

I flew into Seoul, South Korea and met with several nice people who were manufacturing products that had some interest to me. They wanted to be sure that I was very happy during my visit, and set me up with a charming young lady who stayed with me morning, noon, and night the whole time I was there. I must say she helped make the trip very pleasant. While in Korea, I went down to the south of the country on a very small, twin-engine plane

Boarding a plane became as routine to Randy as hopping in a car. (Scandinavian Airlines System)

to see one of the mills. It's interesting that the equipment in most of the plants I visited was all brand new and German, very up-to-date and well-priced for the market. On the way back to Seoul, the door of the plane just flipped open, and for a few minutes, I thought the world had just come to an end. We managed to land safely, and luck surely helped a lot on that day.

From there, I headed to Japan and, my, it was a very different world in 1967. It was exciting, and everyone was very kind to me, as they showed me all the products that could be made. The price was exciting too, so I headed home with my head filled with new ideas and things that could be done to enhance our product lines.

When I started working at Bates in 1965, I was wearing two hats, as head of the design department and the assistant national sales manager. This really kept me on the go, and there just seemed to be so much happening at the time. There were days when I would just sit in my office and wonder if I was in over my head, doubting whether I would survive it all.

The national sales manager was one of the brightest men I have ever known, and he handled that job with such ease. There was just one major problem: He was an alcoholic. Since I really was not a drinker, I did not realize what I had gotten myself tied to, and foolishly thought that I could help him. Now I realize that the situation was way beyond me, and to really be a help to someone, you need professional intervention. Sadly, no one really wanted to take the time to help him out, not even his own family. They really didn't want to think about it, and hoped that it would clear up, and all would be fine.

We went to Japan together on business. Even though he

would drink himself blind every night, he would be up in the morning before me and ready to get things done. On the way home from Japan we stopped in Hawaii, and low and behold, he went on a drunk. I couldn't find him for three days, and when I did, he was in no shape to come home. He was all tied up with a "lady of the night." I told him I was going home, as I needed my job, and they were going to be really hot under the collar at the office, wondering where we were. He managed to get through that episode, but my business life seemed to increase its pace after that.

When I finally arrived home, I walked into the office and the receptionist welcomed me back. I looked at her, handed her a card, and she broke up laughing as it was all in Japanese. I had gotten so many cards while in Japan, I just handed them out. Every time someone said "Welcome home," I would bow and hand them a card. It was just the clown in me, I guess.

I flew back to Japan about six months later, to try to develop some of the products I saw there on my first trip, and I learned a lot about traveling as it took nineteen hours to fly from New York to Osaka. When I arrived, I could not remember if it was morning or night as I was so out of it. All these Japanese gentlemen greeted me at the airport, and each wanted to carry something for me. I gave one my hat, another, my briefcase, and so on until I had nothing to carry. They asked how the trip was, and I told them that I was very tired. They said, "What you need is a massage," and they set one up for me the moment I got to the hotel. You must understand that I had never had a massage, so little did I know what I was in for.

There was a very nice young actress who showed me to a room, told me to take off my clothes, gave me a towel, told

Mabel Trull, Shirley Zapphro (center), and Randy enjoy an evening in Osaka, Japan. "I told Mother," said Randy, "just dress for comfort. We'll be sitting on the floor."

me to put it around me, and after we walked about twenty feet, she took the towel off me. Then she stuck me in a huge, heated machine that had a place for my neck, but my head was hanging outside. She cooked me good, then she told me to sit on this little stool that was about four inches off the floor. I was stark naked, and she threw buckets of cold water at me — not what I would call the thrill of a lifetime.

After all this, she had me lie on the table where she poured oil on me, and began to rub me all over. I don't care who you are or what you like, this was a real turn-on, but she managed that fine. When I finally came out, they asked me how I felt, and I told them that I would have to go right to bed as now I was really worn out, both physically and emotionally.

After that first evening's wildness, I went up by train into the mountains outside of Osaka to what is just a small mill town. I was met at the station by the owner of the mill and his two sons, and he reminded me of someone that I had seen in old movies with a great smile, but he had a mouthful of gold teeth. He was a manufacturer of cotton velvet rugs, and I thought that if he had those wide looms, then I could have him make bedspreads that would look like a cut velvet lid, and would have a whole new look for Bates. This was a fun project, and I had a ball doing it while seeing a new place. Ultimately, the ideas worked, since Bates brought out an entire line of the spreads. Then Randy was off to dream up something else.

The man who owned the mill was the biggest chicken farmer in Japan and served in the parliament, but the velvet mill was his hobby. When we got into the car, I noticed that the windows had little curtains on it so that you could not see who was in the car. There had been some real social unrest, so this was probably a good idea. Son number one rode with us in the front car, while son number two rode in the car behind us as we went to the mill.

When we arrived, they took off their shoes, so I did the same, but my feet were too big for the slippers so I walked around in my socks. Just think about this for a minute: This was a velvet mill, so and there were many different dyes used. Since I was in my socks, these soaked through and turned my feet different colors! Oh well, I wanted to get on with my latest idea, so no worrying about my feet at this point.

I stayed at the owner's home, and it was really very nice, but very strange to me, as I was an occidental, not an oriental. His wife and daughter never spoke to me; they just crawled in and out of the rooms as they served us dinner, drinks, or whatever else we wanted. Son number two ate in the room next to us; son number one was allowed to eat with us. Going to my room to sleep was another mad feeling. The room had a console television and that was all, except beautiful paintings hanging on the walls, a pad in the middle of the room with two pillows, and that was it. Quite a different culture than what I was used to in the West.

1968 was a busy year for me, and I traveled all over the world while thinking up new ideas, trying to make them work. I went back to Japan that year, but took my mother as she loved to travel, and said, "Let's go around the world, via Japan." We stopped in Hong Kong, and from there she wanted to go to Iran, as she really wanted one of those Persian rugs, so we made all the plans. I told her that she was going to have a problem in Japan as they would want us to eat on the floor, it took forever, and she was going to have to deal with the corset she wore as support.

It was very hard for her to sit on the floor with it, so we came up with the great idea that she would have dresses made in the empire style, with the waist just under the breast, and a full skirt below. That way she would not have to wear her corset. Well, we had a great time, and I took my assistant with me as I was now printing an entire line of spreads in Japan, and needed some help.

During the day, mother would go out and do her thing. At one point, she wanted to play golf and the mill people set it up for her to play in Kyoto. She had a lady caddie who had a mouth full of gold teeth and she would smile every time mother hit the ball. She would ask her, "Where is the green on this hole," and the caddie would smile and point straight down. This meant that you had to hit the ball thirty yards out, and hope that it would fall straight down. At the next hole she pointed up, and mother learned to hit it straight up, and hope it would stop in the right spot. If she missed, the caddie would just smile and patiently put down another ball. This certainly was different from the courses in Raleigh. After this experience, she said that golf had a new meaning!

We flew from Japan to Hong Kong, and stayed a few days while mother had enough clothes made for the queen of Sheba. That went well, and we headed for Afghanistan, landing in India during a refueling. When we landed in Teheran, we headed for the Hilton where we stayed. She was less than thrilled with the rug idea as she was not convinced that she was really getting what she wanted. To tell the truth I knew nothing about the rug business, so I left it up to her. It was so hot there that you could not swim in the pool until late in the evening, and even then, it was just like a warm bath. I don't think we were as thrilled as we should have been, but seeing the crown jewels and the peacock throne was something to remember for the rest of your life.

Istanbul was our next stop, and nothing was really very exciting there except going to the Kasbah and watching mother trying to deal with the Turks. Some of them were eyeing me, and I am still not sure what they had in mind. Maybe they were interested in this American woman who seemed so sure of herself. Anyway, I just stood back and watched her deal with them. After all this, the rest of the trip was not that exciting as we both had been all over Europe before, so it was just a rerun of some of the things we had seen.

Fall of 1968 seemed to be going great, and I guess as we all do, I just did not think that things could change in a

"Dressed in their own distinctive styles, a happy foursome of Randy Trull, Marie Pulusty, Ray Tenerello, and Marsha Franklin glides along the ice at the benefit skating party," read the cutline for this photo in *Newsday*, December 11, 1967.

moment. One Saturday afternoon in early September, I was out visiting a friend in the Hamptons. I was washing my car, and Jack came out into the yard and said that I had a phone call. I answered, and to my surprise, it was my mother's closest friend Josephine Stevens. I could tell by the sound of her voice that something was wrong, and my mind went to my grandparents who I knew she was very close to. I was sure that something had happened to one of them, but she started talking very slowly and said that she had some sad news for me and then in the next moment she said that my brother, Jim, had died about three o'clock that afternoon.

I just stood there thinking it can't be, he is only thirty-nine years old—there must be a mistake! It was for real, and then she talked about my coming right home. Then my mother got on the phone. She seemed so calm, as she tried to keep focused on what I should do, and told me that I must come home. I put the phone in Jack's hand. As he heard the news, he told them that he would help me get there as soon as possible.

A thousand things went through my mind, but Jack really took control and started making phone calls planning how to get me home, while I just sat there and let them set things up to get me back to New York, and then on the plane to Raleigh. Dad met me at the airport, and we drove right to Jim's house, where I joined in, trying to get things done that seemed important at that moment.

To this point, I have not said much about Jim, but he had a super nice wife named Juanita. They had two little girls: Holly, who was seven, and Cathy, who was ten. We all thought about the children, and how to deal with this situation that would make it easier for them, since they were so small and fragile. We decided that I would take them down to the funeral home and let them see that their Daddy was just asleep. I walked into the chapel and I did not take them up to the front, but just stood in the back with them and told them he had gone to sleep. You could see him from there, and I felt it was better not to stand up in front as I am not sure, but I think at that point it was harder on me. At that age, they just did not realize what had happened.

The next few days were not easy for anyone, but mother took control of things and planned it out, always thinking of the children and what she thought was best for them. I always said she was a strong lady who seemed to deal with this type of thing very well. Certain times call for you to react in certain ways, but when the shock and services are over, you then begin to see how you really handle things. This was when I found out that mother was going out to the cemetery every day to just sit.

I thought that I must stop her from doing this, but when I talked with her, she was calm, and said, "Son, you must understand that when Jim died, a part of me died with him.

I put my life on the line to bring you two into this world, and I will not have any more children. Although your father is special and I love him, if something happens to him I might meet someone else, but I will never have any other children with anyone else. So I sit here, just to feel close to Jim. I will go on, and in time this will pass, but never be forgotten."

As it turned out, 1969 was a year of change for me, but it did not happen until right at the end of the year. I was very busy at Bates, wearing two hats, and trying to think of things that were new and exciting. But dealing with our national sales manager was a real challenge. It was in late December when he went on one of his alcohol binges, and no one knew where he was. I was covering for him at the office hoping that someone would find him.

Three days before Christmas, I was sitting in my office when the phone rang and there was a very nice man on the phone from J.P. Stevens who wanted to know if I would be interested in joining Stevens. I laughed a little, thanked him, but said "No thank you."

Just two hours later the president of Bates called me into his office and proceeded to tell me that I was the best designer in the industry, but I was fired since I was on Bill Johnson's team. Bill was, himself, going to be fired when he finally showed up. At that moment, I think I knew for sure that I was not a politician, as I could not believe what I heard. One must accept things, so I left his office in shock, and hardly knew what to do. I headed back to my office, called the gentleman at Stevens, and told him that I had changed my mind. I said that I thought that it would be interesting to join his organization, and we talked about my starting there.

I was taken aback, as it was the first time I had been fired, and it surely took some steam out of my sails. I started packing my personal things into boxes and asked my secretary to come in and watch what I was doing. I wanted to be sure that someone knew I was only taking my personal things. I sealed the boxes, wrote my name across the seal, then locked the office and gave her my key.

As I packed for a trip home to see my parents, I got a call from the controller who told me that they were giving me three weeks salary, and that he wanted to get into my office. I told him that the secretary had the key, but told him that if he touched one of those boxes signed and sealed without my being there, I would sue them. Then I wished him a nice Christmas, and headed out the door for North Carolina.

"What's in a Room?" was the working title of a daytime TV show pilot producers hoped to launch in 1968, with Randy as a star designer. The project was ahead of its time and Fred Silverman at CBS turned it down.

After the holidays, I headed back to the city and went to the office where I held a meeting with the chairman of the board. I told him that I did not want him to try to reverse their decision, but I wanted the severance pay term changed to six months. I felt sure that he was not going to argue with me, so I asked him to call in the controller and the president. When they arrived, I told them that I would be leaving, but the chairman agreed that I should be paid for six months, not three weeks. The controller looked like he was having a stroke, but I told him to please make out the check and that I would be out of here. Since I did not trust him, I went straight across the street to the bank and cashed the check.

Well, life does not end with just one job or career or even with a loved one's death, so you have to think about what is next. One of the things that I have always tried to do is think forward, not look back at history. I realized then that I must think of what I would do and where I would go in my life.

A Fascination with Boats

ABOUT 1960, I CAME TO realize that I have had more than a passing fascination with one particular "toy." Boats, particularly motor-cruisers and yachts, have been a part of who I am and where I escape to since that time. To this very day, I still find an immediate release when I come aboard and enter my own private world. Here I can enjoy the water, the beach views, and can have a chance to let my imagination run. I might redecorate, entertain, or just relax. My boat is, and has been for many years, my favorite place to be.

Why I first jumped into the male-dominated realm that is the boating world, I am not quite sure, but I have been a part of that costly fraternity for the last forty-five years. I bought my first boat about 1963 or 1964, and I must have kept it about two years. Then I bought the Luhrs in 1966, and moved to the Wheeler in 1968. I kept that one until about 1974, and then purchased a 34-foot Hatteras in 1975. I jumped from this to a 47-foot Chris Craft in 1977, which I kept it until the early '80s, and I bought the big Hatteras in Florida in about 1984 or 1985. I still have the 53-foot Hatteras today, and it is sitting in Charleston. I try to go there as much as possible for that reason.

It is hard to remember just when I got all involved in boating, but I think I bought the first boat in Norwalk, Connecticut. It was a 25-foot Chris Craft, and you would think that I had just bought the Queen Mary. I bought it with a friend of mine whose name was Tony Putnam, actually Harrington Putman the third, I think — but who really cares? He was just friend of mine at the time, and he was not really that important to me.

The boat that we bought was a real joke, as I really did not know much about boating. Tony had sailed a little, so he surely knew more than I did, but that is not saying much for either of us. We decided to head off on a trip for two weeks, and our goal was to go to Newport, Rhode Island. The first stop was going to be Oyster Bay, and since I knew little about channels, I just ran it the way I thought we should go. Well, I quickly learned that I was not right, and I managed to tear a hole in the bottom, but I was close enough to the marina that they saved the boat. They took it out of the water, and said to come back tomorrow, and they would have it ready for us to keep going. The only thing that they did not say was how much it was going to cost. The next day when I wrote the check, I began to understand what J.P. Morgan said: "When you have to ask how much it will cost, then you can't afford it." In our case, that cost was a boat!

When we went up to Newport, Rhode Island, we tied up to a boat that made ours look like a row boat. This nice lady leaned over the side and said, "What a cute little boat!"

Realizing who she was, Tony replied, "Thank you, Mrs. Trask." It turns out, she knew Tony and his family, and invited us up on her enormous boat to have drinks. At least at that moment, I felt special.

Life moves on, and Tony and I parted ways, so I bought him out of the boat. I then sold it and bought a new, 28-foot Luhrs. Man, did I think it was great. It had room to sleep four, and a small bath with no shower, but what did it matter? I had arrived with a new boat.

Young Randy, in his natural element.

We took off from Norwalk, Connecticut and headed to Fire Island, New York to show off what, to me, was a grand boat. The problem turned out to be that I read the maps wrong, and we went the wrong way for hours before I figured out which way to go. By then, it was getting late and dark so I headed for a small harbor on the north shore, and planned to stay there for the night, and start out tomorrow for Fire Island. When we got into the harbor, the marina was closed, so we tied up right on the gas dock. I told Ed he could sleep in the forward cabin and I would sleep on the dinette table, which turned into a bed. Off to sleep we went at about 12:30.

Early the next morning, a crowd of local fishermen arrived on the dock and one of them said "What in the hell is this?"

With that, Ed boomed out, "It's the Queen Mary. What the hell did you think it is?" Ed had one of those very deep voices that sounded like a truck driver. When I looked through the curtains, the locals were so surprised that they almost fell off the dock. That voice and the timing really had its effect!

We arrived at Fire Island around five o'clock, and everyone was sitting out on the dock drinking. I put my battery-run record player on the bridge and was playing Auntie Mame when a boat that cut in front of us stopped suddenly. I quickly tried to throw the boat into reverse, but it was frozen in forward, so I shot forward. With that crowded harbor, I just picked out which boat I was going to hit, as there was no way to stop the collision, and went. The record player hit the deck with a crash, and we crashed straight into the smaller boat that had cut us off. When I rode up on the side of that boat, everyone on the dock started to applaud the landing. I just wanted to disappear, but there was no chance.

Oh well, it was a new way to land the boat, and not what I wanted. All I could think of was that my new boat was banged up, but in truth, it really didn't do much damage, and no one was hurt. The company that sold me the boat took care of everything, and did this pretty quickly. Oh boating, what fun if you are mad!

I only kept that boat a couple of years, but then I had a chance to buy a 40-foot Wheeler. It was a really old boat, but bigger, and I fell in love with it. It also gave me a chance to start all over, outfitting the boat the way I wanted to. I had to put new engines in the boat since they were shot, and I wanted a generator installed so that I could have power, even if I was just at anchor, without draining the batteries.

The first weekend after they put in the generator, I headed off to Oyster Bay to a little cove where lots of beautiful sailboats go in the evening and drop anchor. I did the same thing, and just dropped anchor where it suited me. I turned on my generator, set up a sewing machine on the back deck, and started making the curtains for the boat. As far as I was concerned, this seemed like a great place, but the other boaters were aghast. I sat there sewing away, and the noise did not please them. What the hell: you can't please everyone, and I needed to get those curtains made!

I ultimately named the boat *The Constantine*, and put Athens under the name. What fun I had with that. As I was coming into the harbor in Connecticut one time, I heard some man call out to his friend, "Did you see that boat? It is from Athens."

The other man with him said, "Hell, that boat could not have come from Athens."

I smiled and said, "Yes it could—Georgia." And they both broke up laughing.

This was not the only time this happened. Sometime later on, I was sitting in Sayville, Long Island when a lady came walking down the dock, stopped, and said, "My, look at this boat—they must be Greek. The boat is all done in the Greek colors, and it is from Athens." To tell the truth, I did not even know that blue and white were the Greek colors, I just liked them.

I smiled and said, "Yes, I am Greek."

"How long did it take you to get here from Greece?" she asked.

I told her, "I've been cruising for years, and just stopped for a motor job." What a line this was, and she went for it.

Not long after this, some man came walking along the dock and said, "Boy, what kind of engines do you have in that boat?" He was fat and ugly, with a big cigar hanging out of his mouth. First, I did not like being called boy, and second, I don't know anything about engines, I just want them to run.

I looked straight at him and said "They are blue to match the carpet." That cigar fell right out of his mouth!

Owning this boat was great, but some things I did not plan on, happened. One was that the marine authorities said you were required to have a holding tank for the toilet, but there were very few places that you could empty it. One day, we were sitting on the boat drinking and a friend of mine who drinks too much asked what I was going to do since the holding tank was full. I really did not have an answer, so he just looked at me and said, "Oh I will take care of it for you. Just put the container in a garbage bag and I will take it over to the bar, and pour it down the toilet." It sounded like a great idea, and he left the boat with the bag full of you know what, and we waited for him to come back. After a while, we wondered what could have happened to him, so we walked over to the bar. There he sat, drunk as could be, with that bag full of shit. We broke up laughing, thinking what in the world would people say if they knew what he had in that bag. We all just fled to the boat, and wished him the best.

It came time to move on with a larger boat, so I found a 34-foot Hatteras. To me, that was the last word in boats, so I sold the Wheeler, and bought the Hatteras. Not a lot happened on that boat, but I enjoyed it in the summer. Since it was fiberglass, I didn't have to spend all winter working on the hull either; I just washed and cleaned it off for another fun time after each use.

My next transition came when I saw a 47-foot Chris Craft in the marina. It was a really great boat, but the owner had a sudden heart attack, and it was for sale. I decided that it was for me, so I sold mine, and bought his. A 47-foot-long boat is no longer just a toy. Now I was into real boating with the big shots, and I decided to take the boat to Florida for the winter. I lined up friends to help me take it down, and since no one person could take off the amount of time it would take me to get it down, several friends made up different parts of the trip.

One of my oldest friends, Pat Clay, lived in Norfolk, Virginia, and was with me on a trip down the Chesapeake Bay. As we moved closer to where the Potomac River joins the Chesapeake, he was reading from the regional marine chart book. He remarked that it said if there was a northeast wind in that area, it would make you wish you had never seen the Potomac River. At just about that moment, we were maybe twenty minutes away from where the river entered the bay. Suddenly, the boat began to yaw, going all over the place, and smoke came up from below.

We thought the boat was on fire, so I did the sort of thing

Edward Lee Cave was a major player in New York real estate, and a good friend of mine. He has that Kennedy-style smile.

a good captain would do: I went to the radio and called the Coast Guard. I didn't know all the things you were supposed to say, so I just said, "Mayday, Mayday" into the radio microphone.

The responder asked, "Are you sinking!"

I answered, "May is just around the corner, and day is coming up!"

He broke out laughing. The man on the radio said that would go down in his log book, as it was something he'd never heard before. All I was trying to tell them was if that damn thing was on fire, I was leaving!

The problem turned out to be steam from one of the engines that had overheated. When I turned that engine off, it stopped the steam smoke. The Coast Guard patrol boat came alongside, and they escorted us into a local marina, where it turned out to be no big deal. The ultimate outcome of that trip was fine—the boat arrived in Coconut Grove, and everything that had gone on didn't seem to matter.

All my life, I had wanted a 53-foot Hatteras and thought if I could have that boat, the world would come to an end. Now that I was making enough money for something like this, I was always on the lookout for my dream boat. One Friday afternoon, I was shown one and I thought it was just what I wanted.

When I got back to the Chris, it was about seven o'clock, and we sat and had a few drinks. I then decided that was the boat I wanted, so I picked up the phone and called Frank Gordon who had shown it to me. As luck would have it, he was still in his office so I told him to give the owner an offer of $200,000. He said they were asking $260,000. I told him to make the offer, and we'll just see what they say.

Within ten minutes, he called back and said they would take $220,000. Big Mouth Trull said, "Well, call them back and tell them $210,000.

He told me I was crazy, and reminded me that they had just come down forty thousand. Now, I wanted them to come down ten more.

I laughed and said, "Well, if you don't want to do it, just give me the number and I will call."

At that point, he realized how stubborn I was and gave up. Another ten minutes went by, and he called me back. He said that he could not believe it, but that they had said yes to the offer.

He reminded me that this was all subject to a survey, and my getting the loan, however. I laughed when he said this, and said, "Tell them not to worry. I will pay cash for the boat." At this point, Frank seemed a little shocked, but said nothing. Later, he told a friend of mine that it was the first boat he had ever sold where there was no loan involved somewhere in the purchase.

The next morning, the phone rang and a man started talking to me about the Hatteras. This fellow had been told that I had bought the boat for $210,000 and that he would give me $250,000 to not take it, as he really wanted the boat. I said, "Thank you, but no thank you. I have waited for years for this boat, and now it's mine."

After my purchase, I used the boat as often as possible. I would take the boat to the New York area for the summer, then back down to Florida for the winter. I have no idea how many times I made that trip, but it seemed that I was on the move all the time. My dear friend, Rosita Fanto, commented one time that I spent most of my time going back and forth, since it took about two weeks to make the trip. I had to plan it all out, and I would make sure that I had friends to visit along the way. Some of those same people would occasionally come and stay onboard with me, as I moved up and down the coast. Kind of fun, but lots of planning involved in all that.

I had it in New York for the big rededication of the Statue of Liberty. There were over forty thousand other boats in the harbor around lower Manhattan, and I wanted to entertain, rather than deal with all that myself. I wanted to have Ray, the man I used to captain the boat when I did not run it myself, handle the boat for me. He had recently brought the boat up from Florida for me, with help from his son. Because I had to be in Europe for a major design show just prior to this event, I just told him to deliver it.

We got together after he was there with the boat, and had a great time. I was lucky that a friend of mind had connections

at the Brooklyn Navy Yard. We were able to leave it moored
there during a time when there was no other slip space to be
found in the entire New York or New Jersey coastal area.
Ray took us out for the festivities, and I had about twenty-
five friends as guests nearly every day and evening. This
made it great fun, and there was no work for me.

One particular event on that boat stands out in my memory, however. Some friends and I went for a cruise up the
Hudson River, and had quite an evening. We were drinking
and carrying on, so we dropped anchor near the Manhattan
power station to be near the Fourth of July fireworks, but
get out of the busy main channel and have a view of the
city. Not long after this, a U.S. Coast Guard patrol boat
pulled alongside and gave us a stern warning about being in
a restricted area. As it turned out, we had dropped anchor
right where the main power cable for all of Manhattan was
located. We immediately began to hoist the anchor, prepar-
ing to move on, but were in for a surprise.

As the anchor came closer and closer to the surface, one
of my friends yelled, "Hold on! There's something caught
on the anchor!"

We all looked at each other and said, almost together,
"Oh S — — —!" It turned out that we had snagged the main
power cable, and were winching it aboard on the anchor.
There was enough power going through that cable to fry the
entire boat, not to mention all of us. Luckily, we managed to
cut away the anchor line, release the chain, and move the R.
Trull just enough to detach the power line. We then slipped
away, unharmed.

I was lucky that time, and many others, but I have learned
much about boating over the years. Whoever thought a designer could really run a boat? I often prove these doubters

Randy Trull

Above: The 34-foot double cabin Hatteras.

Below: Randy decorated his '47 Criscraft Commando in red, white, and blue in hopes of winning the decorator prize at a 1970s Fire Island Fourth of July Celebration. "It was a rainy, dreamy day," Randy reminisced. "We just kept right on decorating, regardless, because I wanted to win that prize, and I did."

wrong! To this day, however, no one really believes that I am capable of running a large boat. These same folks sit there in utter shock when I handle it like it is a toy, and have no problem. Although I can manage a boat, I have also learned when to give up control to a professional. As I became older and wiser, I often used a hired captain. An example of this was during Ronald Reagan's second inauguration.

This was in 1982, and there were thousands of other boaters trying to get into the right place at the right time for the festivities. The Potomac River is tidal, and pretty busy anyway, but it was really packed then. Considering the crowd, the alcohol involved in many of those onboard parties and the general carelessness which many boaters exhibit, that captain really kept us out of trouble.

6 | *Surviving the Seventies*

SINCE I WAS FIRED from Bates in December of 1969, and did not work for a specific firm until the late spring of 1970, I had some time to travel and consider my situation and goals. Changing a career, and really just starting over, can be a bit of a trauma, but remember that I had six month's salary to decide what I wanted to do and how to do it, so there was no real pressure for me. One of the offers for a new job was from J. P. Stevens, and it sounded really good.

They invited me to lunch at the Harvard Club, and at lunch they made me an offer. At the time, that seemed really great, but as I got more into the proposal, I was told I would have to report to a guy who was two years younger than me and that he had no experience in the business. He was a graduate of Harvard or Yale, but I was sure that I could leave him standing at the starting gate. I told the bosses that I would bury this guy in a month and I was willing to work with him, but not under him. I had lunch with the managers there three times, and the boss at Stevens said that was the last lunch until I made my mind up, which I did the next day. I told him, "No, thank you."

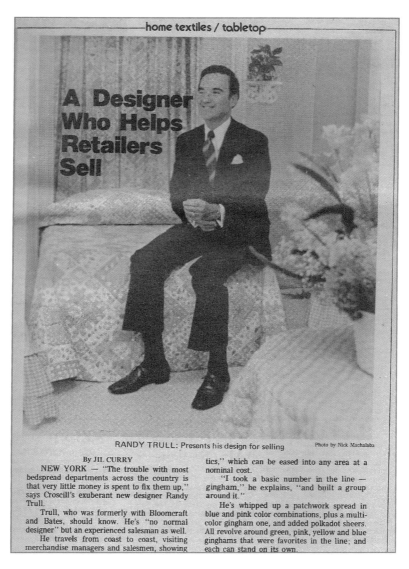

— home textiles / tabletop —

A Designer Who Helps Retailers Sell

RANDY TRULL: Presents his design for selling

Photo by Nick Machalaba

By JIL CURRY

NEW YORK — "The trouble with most bedspread departments across the country is that very little money is spent to fix them up," says Croscill's exuberant new designer Randy Trull.

Trull, who was formerly with Bloomcraft and Bates, should know. He's "no normal designer" but an experienced salesman as well.

He travels from coast to coast, visiting merchandise managers and salesmen, showing tics," which can be eased into any area at a nominal cost.

"I took a basic number in the line — gingham," he explains, "and built a group around it."

He's whipped up a patchwork spread in blue and pink color combinations, plus a multi-color gingham one, and added polkadot sheers. All revolve around green, pink, yellow and blue ginghams that were favorites in the line; and each can stand on its own.

Over 18 million yards of fabric have sold that bear Randy Trull designs. At one time, bedspreads and pillows he designed were in more than 3.5 million homes in the United States.

In the spring of 1970, I was living on Park Avenue and sharing the apartment with Jack Rogers. If there was ever an odd couple, we were it. We had a live-in housekeeper named Hazel who had come out of the old school of what a gentlemen should live like, and it was a matter of my adjusting to her, as she was not about to change. We were to eat a five-course meal in the dining room under candlelight, and if I wanted to eat on a tray in my room, then I must be sick, so I got chicken soup. I learned quickly that the kitchen was a weapon, and that what she said was the rule. Because of this, sometimes I would call and tell her that I was on a diet, and all I wanted for dinner was a hamburger and a green salad. She would say, "Fine," and I would arrive home, put on my robe, and she put on her uniform. Then I would eat dinner in the dining room where I would have a five-course meal, two courses of which were hamburger and a green salad. She always served apple sauce (that I never ate), but I later found out that she liked it, and did not have many teeth, so it was easy for her to eat.

Jack was from New England, and a good cook. He had his way of doing things, and Hazel had hers, so I just laughed and watched. One day he told Hazel to take the string beans and just put them in boiling water for four or five minutes, not her usual style of three hours slowing simmering in fat back. She didn't think much of that. At one of Jack's very proper dinner parties, everyone was dressed for the opera, so it was a really stiff sort of dinner. I had just joined the group, and was not going to the opera, but was witness to one of Hazel's moods.

When Hazel served the string beans that night, they looked horribly limp. He looked at them and with a little bit of anger, and said, "What did you do to the string beans?"

Without taking a breath, she just looked at him and said, "I did exactly what you told me to do. I put them into boiling water for four or five minutes, then I cooked them." At that point, the dinner party guests just broke up in laughter as Hazel had put him straight. He really did not have much to say after that, but everyone seemed to enjoy the moment. I guess I did the same.

Not long after this Hazel story, I had a call from an acquaintance I made in England named Basel Glass. He was in New York with his wife, and he said that he would like to talk to me about the possibility of working for him in England, where he was the head of Vantona, a fabric company. I invited the two of them for dinner, but it turned out a little strange as I was I trying to "put on the dog" a little.

Mrs. Glass, who lived at that time in Monte Carlo, thought she was a bit grand. As the dinner progressed, she kept going on and saying how delicious everything was, so I thought I would try and take a little starch out of her. When Hazel served the dessert, Mrs. Glass again told me how delicious it was. I just laughed, and said that it was my mother's favorite recipe: black cherry Jell-O, made with Coca Cola. I thought she was going to drop dead right there, but it certainly added to the evening, and Basel offered me a consulting job with Vantona, which I accepted. Now I would be able to work in England, and that was a whole new challenge.

Sitting at home with a live-in housekeeper, and having little to do, was not really my style, but I was on the phone and talking with lots of people, looking for what I thought was the right job for me. One day, the phone rang, and to my surprise, it was Louis Bloom. He said he had heard I was not working. He was being very nice, but did not say much, so I asked if he had something in mind. He said he did not spend a dime for nothing, which really made me mad, so I asked what he had in mind. He indicated that he would be interested in my joining Bloomcraft, a Fabric House.

I said if he wanted to talk with me, he could come to my apartment a week from tomorrow at five o'clock, to which he agreed. The funny part is that I really had nothing to do between the time of the telephone conversation and the time I made up, I was just being a pain as I did not like the way he talked to me. I must give him credit through, as he arrived right on time, was charming, and made me a very nice offer. My opportunity to join Bloom's firm came as a surprise to me, as I had known him for years and did not really think a lot of him during that time. Sometimes when you don't really know people you form opinions which are not always right.

I told him that I would give his offer some thought, and would give him a call next week, which I did. I told him I would like to have another talk, thinking that he would ask me to come to the office, but to my surprise he said that he would come back up to my apartment. Again, we talked for a while, and he made me the same offer. I told him that I was headed for Europe the following week, and that we would get together as soon as I got back.

When I arrived back in New York, I called Louis, and he again came to my apartment. That was when I told him that I had committed to do some work for Basil Glass at Vantona, and that I would work in London about three months a year. At this point, he said that he did not think he should pay what he had offered for my time as he would not have me full time. I agreed, and asked when he would like for me to come to work. At this point, I had not even seen the office, so he said to come down tomorrow and have lunch. Boy that turned out to be a weird day!

After I arrived, we all went to the restaurant. During the meal, he turned to all the gentlemen at the table—two vice presidents and the chairman of the board—and told them to congratulate me as I had just joined the company. I can't describe the look on their faces, as they looked at me like I was something from outer space, but Don Bidle said, "Welcome," and was very nice to me from day one. This began a new adventure for me, and I must say, it was a great chance that he gave.

Those first few months were different from anything I had ever done. I wandered around the office trying to figure out what in the world was I supposed to be doing, since he had never really told me their expectations. Everyone was nice, but no one even asked me to do anything. In pure frustration, I walked into Louis' office one day and told him that I had decided to go to Europe the next week to research what other designers were doing. He said, "Fine" to my utter surprise, as I thought he would tell me things he wanted me to do instead. He called the controller and told him to give me whatever I needed for the trip.

Now that I look back, I realize Louis knew more about me than I thought. I never worked so hard on a trip trying to find new products, while trying to come up with new ideas to use. I must give him credit: He knew me better than I knew myself. I needed the challenge, and he let me try to hang myself, knowing that I would work even harder to succeed and prove my worth. He was a smart man, even though we were never close.

Bloomcraft did make a big change in my life. I was finally

in a company where there were no politics, and I was able to do what I liked because all the bosses would help make it work. I was out in front working with the customers selling, designing and having fun. I guess I was brought out of the closet where most designers were kept. These things made the job great, and Louis let me do the things I needed or wanted to. Most of the time, he was truly nice to me, even though his personality was not very warm. All I had to do to please him was what I thought would help the company, and he would back me all the way.

I did not realize how much of a salesman I was back then, but then again, I did not feel that I was selling. What most people did not realize about me was that what they called "selling" was not what I was doing. I was just confident in my ideas, and in my efforts at design, and truly believed in what I would show or say to the customer. It has been said that a good salesman can sell anything, and I could sell anything that I was a part of. That is where I was very different from the way most salesmen work.

Leaving Bloomcraft was, to say the least, a bit of madness that I am not sure I was prepared for, but I will try to tell it the way it was for me. We were heading into a market week, and Louis had just sold the company. Now the company was full of politics, and I was having a hard time with it. Suddenly, I got a call from a lady whose name was Margaret, and she wanted to know if I would talk to a Mike Kahn, president of Croscill, a home fashion house. She asked me to come to their office on a Thursday evening, right next door to our office.

Let's face it, everyone likes to feel they are special, and having her call me for this meeting made me think I was something special. Whether or not I was really doesn't matter. I went to the meeting and found that Mike was a really strong personality, he was sure that I would accept what he had to offer. We talked, and he offered me a job there. I told him that I wanted to think about it, and that I would let him know on Monday. Since everyone in the industry knew each other, played cards together, talked on the phone and drank together, they knew what was going on all around. With the designers' group, it wasn't so chummy, so all of us were out of the loop.

On Friday, Don Biddle called me into his office. He was the senior vice president at Bloomcraft, and everyone knew he would be president when Louis left. He was a great guy, and I really did like working for him. He said that he had heard that Bloomcraft was going to lose someone that was important to the company, and I said something smart ass, like I hadn't heard anything.

At this point, he said, "Don't play games, you. I know who has made you an offer. What did you tell him?"

At that point I said, "I was going to tell him on Monday."

Don then said, "Well, you are going to mess my weekend up? I want you to stay here."

Monday arrived, and I went into Don's office and told him that I would stay at Bloomcraft if he really wanted me to, but he must take the responsibility for my doing this, as that was the only reason I would stay.

He looked at me smiled and said, "Tell Mike, 'No,' and stay here with me." We both laughed, and I walked out headed for Croscill to tell Mike "No thank you," and boy was that a hard deal for me. He said that Don had talked me out of the move. Since I was looking for some reason to cover my real feelings, I told Mike I had looked at his line and I did not like it. It was not me, and he was telling me what to sell, so I thought I would be wrong for your company. It was just silly talk, and I was just trying to ease out. That was when I realized that all the guys in the business knew each other and played games, because each wanted to win over the other.

On Wednesday of that week, just two days after telling Mike no, I was standing in the showroom at Bloomcraft. Louis and one of the designers whose products we were showing was there in a Pakistani dress, telling me that the way I showed his products looked like something from 125th Street, not Fifth Avenue. Louis was letting him do this, and not defending me since I worked for him. He just stood there, and I just told the guy to do whatever you want, Louis is the boss.

Don, who was standing near me, realized I was upset, and walked over to me. He quietly said, "Kick him in the balls, if you can find them under that dress!"

I broke up laughing, but was mad as hell. I walked straight to my office, called Mike Kahn up, and asked if I could talk to him again. He said, "Yes, but if we agree on the details, there will be no going home to think about it. We will sign this evening." What I did not know was that Mike could not stand to be told no, and he was not about to let Don talk me out of the deal. They were the smart ones, and I was the toy.

I went to Croscill that evening and told Mike that he would have to make me a vice president of the company. He looked a little surprised, as they surely had never had a southern W.A.S.P. as an officer of the company.

He said, "Give me a few minutes," then he left the room. When he returned, he said, "Okay, but you must be here six months before we announce it." That was no problem for me, so we signed an agreement. I then told Mike that since market started on Sunday, and everything that I had done was still at Bloomcraft, he could not say anything until the market closed. Boy was I the dumb one!

He was not taking any chances that Don, or anybody else, was going to talk me out of this. He told me that he was holding his sales meeting at the hotel on Saturday, and asked that I please come and have lunch. When I arrived, he pulled me right to the front told everyone that I was going to be the new designer for Croscill, I was a bit upset as I was, after all, still an employee of Bloomcraft, but Mike was smarter than I was, and he was taking no chances of my changing my agreement. On Monday morning, the first day at the market, I arrived at the office early and packed all the things in my office that were mine. I just knew Louis would be asking me to come to his office, and I wanted to be prepared for whatever was going to happen.

The call came around ten in the morning, and as I headed for Louis' office, Frances Martin, a major buyer was standing in the showroom. She walked over to me, gave me a hug, and said, "I think it is great for you to go to Croscill." My heart just sank as I realized everyone in the market knew this, and man, was Louis going to give me hell.

I walked into his office and sat down in front of him. Before I could even take a breath, he said, "I understand that you are leaving us and going to Croscill. I want to wish you the best of everything, and you can leave now." I sat there stunned, looked at him, and said that I wanted to leave under the best of circumstances, as one never knows when you may have to cross over a bridge again. With that, he came up out of his chair and told me when someone leaves Bloomcraft, they never come back—they are gone forever. Looking rather stunned, I asked him if he wanted me just to walk out the door that minute, but he said I could stay the rest of the day. I got up, walked out into the showroom, and started saying goodbye to the salesmen. One started crying, and what a day it turned out to be, as all the customers who were there started shaking my hand and wishing me the best. I certainly did not expect it to end that way, especially on the first day of market.

A new day began for me that Tuesday—the second day of market—and with it a new career. Now, I stood at Croscill, watching the faces of the buyers and their groups seeing me standing there, while Mike loved the whole thing. In fact, he told me to come to the Croscill dinner that night as they had a major party for the customers. I think it was at a place called Camelot. Abe Kahn was the chairman of the board, and his wife Marion stood at the door to greet everyone.

Mike had entrusted her to my care. Without thinking, I smiled and said what a beautiful dress she had on, and that the skirt was out of one of my fabrics. I went on to say that I had used the same fabric all over my bedroom walls. She reacted with a bit of anger on her face, and said she had bought the dress in Palm Beach. It was quite an auspicious beginning. Just as I started walking away, another designer, whose company was a major customer, arrived. He smiled and told her he had that same fabric all over his bathroom walls. It was quite a beginning for my career at Croscill, and I don't think Marion ever got over the dress comments.

I soon learned that my bosses at Croscill expected me to attend lots of meetings that centered around plans for the next market. I would tell them what I thought, and they would sit there and look at me as if I had just landed from space. It took them about a year to realize that I just might know something about the market and where we should be headed. The first lines I did for them made them sit up and listen to me, but Mike would still fight me on the details. I did not give in.

At one of our planning meetings, Al, vice president of sales, announced the company was going to add a new curtain to the line. As soon as I saw it, I told them it was ugly and that no one was going to buy it. Mike looked at me and said, "You don't understand. I do not run a democracy here. I run a dictatorship. Al and I already have decided this curtain will be in the new line.

I just smiled and said, "Fine, but nobody is going to buy that damn curtain."

They unveiled the curtain at the next market. I made it a point to walk through the showroom with every major customer. When I got to that curtain I would say, "And this is a curtain," and make a face that told them how dreadful

Randy took this photo just after he, Ciro "Chip" Scala, and Mrs. Mike Kahn returned from the Hamptons, in 1974.

I found it to be. Then, I would move to the next item just bubbling with excitement about it. After the market ended, Mike called me into his office and told me I had killed that curtain.

I just smiled and said, "Oh, no one bought it? Well, I told you it was a dog."

He then proceeded to tell me about the new plan. He and Al were going to allow me a vote. The math did not sound good to me. So, pain in the ass that I am, I said, "That won't work because that's two, you and Al, against one."

Finally, Mike agreed to add hot salesman Ciro "Chip" Scala to the new democracy.

"Good," I told them. At least Chip has good taste.

It would not be so easy to say things like this if Croscill had lost business during my time there. Figures showed much to the contrary. When I arrived, Croscill was doing $14 million a year. When I left, they were doing over $100 million. So, it is safe to say I did something right. In addition to my designs, I started traveling more to move and shake our products. I visited major stores and gave lectures on how to decorate, being careful to celebrate Croscill designs.

You learn all kinds of things when you go out and meet the public. My lectures usually drew a hundred to three hundred ladies who were sitting there waiting to hear you tell them just what they wanted to hear. Most of them were not interested in general decorating tips, they just wanted me to address their individual decorating problems. One of my first questions to them was always, "How many of you have a paint chip, piece of carpet, or piece of fabric or wallpaper with you today?" Usually, about ninety percent of them would raise their hand. I would talk to them for about six minutes, then open the floor for questions.

It seems strange to me, but women are not like men in their loyalties. If a woman offends a man in the midst of other men, at least one of them in going to stand up to her, but I almost could have shot one of those women in the foot without upsetting the other women. At each lecture, I set out to offend one woman early in each question and answer period, because I knew that would win over the other 299. For instance, a woman described the interior of her house to me and asked me what I would do about the design. I simply smiled, and said, "Move!" All the other ladies there went wild laughing and saying things like, "Yes, her house sounds awful." Oh well, lose one gain the rest of the audience.

Randy Trull of Croscill:

"Avril in our printed fabrics gives us superior hand... much more body. We get a better finish and a more attractive product all around. More consumers associate the Avril brand with those qualities and have more **confidence** in it than some retailers may realize. It should be promoted more."

AVRIL
THE KEY WORD IS
CONFIDENCE

FMC Fibers

One lecture I gave in Houston, Texas when I was fairly new at Croscill was covered by a local television reporter. I decided to see if I could start a new trend in fashion color while I was being interviewed, so I said that brown was popular now, but

This Sangar-Harris advertisement for Randy and the Croscill Curtain Company is one of hundreds that ran, at various times, in newspapers and magazines across the country. "Bring your decorating problems," read the promo, "so that our well-traveled professional may introduce you to new design techniques."

aqua would take its place. The next day, the style section of the paper said, "Brown Today, Aqua Tomorrow," and orders started pouring into our firm.

While Vice President of the Croscill Curtain Company, Randy continued to do what came naturally. He made it a practice to "go out all over the country and meet consumers face to face."

Let's face the facts. I am a designer who likes a challenge and sometimes I did things at Croscill that did not make Mike happy. When I returned to New York, Mike said, "What the hell were you doing?"

I answered, "I was just trying to start a new trend."

"For Heaven's sake, start it with a color we have!" he said. I just walked away smiling.

One day, Mike lined up an appearance for me at a major show at Dayton Dry Goods in Minneapolis. That was a tremendous company that is known now as Dayton-Hudson. They founded Target. Mike made sure the president of Dayton would be there, but forgot to tell me anything about any of it. The day before I was to speak, I got a call in New York from one of the company officers at Dayton. "When will you be arriving," he asked.

"Arriving for what?" I answered. I put him on hold and ran to Mike's office.

As usual, he just smiled and said, "Sorry, but I know you'll be able to handle it."

The first flight I could book got me to Minneapolis too late to get to Dayton before the program started. When I walked in, I saw three hundred ladies sitting there geared up to hear three lectures. Figuring I might be late, they put me last on the program.

The first speaker was a teacher and the second was a well-known designer. Both of them had their talks so finely tuned they would stop and wait for laughs at the funny parts of their speeches. I really wasn't prepared for the format. When my turn came, I told the audience that designers are not like doctors or lawyers who have set rules, and since I had no rules, I'd decided to offer criticism of the first two talks for my part of the program. "For instance," I said, "this designer has advised you to paint your kitchens in bright, fresh colors like yellow and red. I'm here to tell you that yellow and red are hot colors and a kitchen is already hot, so use cool colors instead." The audience seemed to like me, but I think it is safe to say the designer and teacher did not.

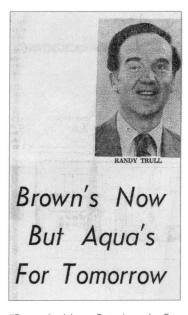

RANDY TRULL

Brown's Now But Aqua's For Tomorrow

"Brown's Now But Aqua's For Tomorrow," screamed the headline in the *Houston Chronicle*. "It was just an off-the-cuff comment I made during a presentation and my boss cussed me out for it, because orders began pouring in immediately, and they had no aqua," said Randy.

Learning how Croscill did business was a new show, and I had to figure out how to make things work for them and work for me. They had a sample room in New York on 25th Street. A lady name Mae ran the sample room and made all the samples for what would become the new line. She was a real jewel who had been with the company for years and knew how to run most of the machines. She made things easier for me at the beginning, but, I decided things would have to go my way. I thought it made perfect sense to move the sample room to the factory. Things would work better with everything in one place, and the factory was located in Durham, NC, just fourteen miles from my home. I could

ABOUT FABRIC

those shibboleths turned out to be nonsense. Surely good design had something to do with the public acceptance of the unconventional, but it was as if the women were expressing a fundamental sense of "I don't know why I like it, but I do." If I have had any success at all, I believe it's because I have always painted "up" to consumers' tastes. In my experience, a woman is apt to buy something that is pretty in patterns she can relate to—flowers and ferns rather than abstract designs. I work in abstractions, love them, but as a nature buff, I first started working with simple nature forms—I've made the lady bug my trade mark—and now I'm coming back to nature subjects because there's an increasing interest in them, especially among young people and I think we have to look to them for inspiration. I'm impressed with what I see them doing—experimenting with color, making cushions out of towels and curtains out of sheets, creating their own backgrounds, not being afraid to change. They are not pushed by convention; they follow their own instincts, which is what I wish people of all ages would feel freer to do. We should all be a little daring in

3 I feel that it's part of my job as a designer to go out all over the country and meet consumers face to face, answering their questions. I generally find that I am face to face with their paint chips and carpet swatches, handbags full of them, because the usual decorating approach is to choose wall and carpet colors and then, as a second or third thought, select the fabrics for a room. That is not as it should be—a room should be planned as a unit, all parts considered as a whole, even if you have to do the job in stages. Paint and carpet first, and you will have locked yourself in. If you come upon a fabric you love that may suggest a different color approach—for instance, in curtains, draperies or a ready-to-put-on-the-bed bedspread, which are my products—you can always, of course, repaint the walls

"today two patterns in a bedspread is high fashion... ten years ago it was a job lot"

3 RANDY TRULL
Vice President, Croscill Curtai[n]
who makes ready-mades look custo[m]

Randy drew many of his ideas from face-to-face meetings with homeowners around the country. "I feel it's part of my job," he said, during his tenure as Vice President of the Croscill Curtain Company. This photo was taken at his 57th Street apartment.

NY Designer Captivates Woman's Club

By NANCY JOLLY

"Though most women are capable of coordinating their wardrobe, they are unable to use their design sense on a larger scale in their homes," contends R. Holland Trull.

The son of Mr. and Mrs. W. E. Trull of Creedmoor Road, the New York designer captivated the group as he dispelled members of the Raleigh Woman's Club at yesterday's luncheon meeting of the Home Life Department.

"You can coordinate the furnishings and colors in your home just as easily as you put together a fashionable outfit," Trull contended. Illustrating his theory was mannequin Cindy Smith wearing fashions and accessories from Burton's.

Trull explained that the decorator chooses colors and patterns to accent a room in the same way that a woman would choose a hat or jewelry to accent her dress.

"The accent color should be placed here and there throughout the room, rather in just one screaming spot of color," he said.

Starting with a floor plan

R. Holland Trull illustrates design techniques with mannequin Cindy Smith.

"I married an industry," Randy said, looking back on six decades of work. He designed and decorated rooms that have been featured in *House and Garden*, *Interior Design*, *Brides*, *Seventeen*, *Good Housekeeping*, *Better Homes and Gardens*, *Ladies Home Journal*, and *House Beautiful*.

In 1975, *House Beautiful* said that "Randy Trull is one of the six most important textile designers in the United States."

spend more time in North Carolina and get the job done at the same time.

Sometimes things seem easy at first, then prove a little stickier. Trying to set up a sample room at the factory was one of those things. I had never thought through certain aspects of moving the sample room to Durham. Herb Schwartz, the plant manager, was a hard and strong New Yorker. He worked all the time at keeping production numbers up and shipping problems down. He had no patience with employees who wasted company time.

Then Randy arrived on the scene, and, soon after, a war started. Croscill built my new sample room on one side of the factory. I had two doors, one from the street and one that led into the factory. This was fine with me because it made it so easy to wander out into the factory and talk to the ladies there. They just loved this nice southern boy chatting with them, but Herb did not like it one bit. He wanted those machines running all the time and he did not want me slowing down production. A few weeks after I started work there, I headed out for lunch and when I came back, Herb had had the interior door of my sample room cemented closed so that the only way that I could get into the plant was to go outside and walk around the entire building. "What a pain in the ass he is," I thought, and he was probably thinking the exact same words.

Herb was always worrying about shipments and production and I was always thinking about new looks and new items. When I came up with a design, that meant he would have to come up with ways to make it. Things that would slow down existing production lines were not very high on his list of priorities. Man, did we fight about that!

I put in an order for new ninety-inch tablecloths and Herb seemed all right with that. Then, one day, I was looking at the open order files and found that every one of those ninety-inch cloths was on "back order," which meant he was not making them. I started screaming at him and he just smiled and said, "Yes, I told you that you could put the design in the line but I did not say that I was going to make them if they slowed down my scheduled production." Oh, what a war we had!

Over time, Herb and I somehow worked through all that. He learned my ways and I learned his, and had an edgy peace at work, but the truth is that we became great friends out of the office. Herb became a good friend of my father's too, and when Herb would run into dad in Raleigh he said that my father would greet him, "So, how is the worry wart?"

Socially, those years at Croscill were fun. I like those things that were happening in my life, that kept me on the move, and that put me out in front of the public. My favorite photo from that time was of me and Marie, a really close friend, ice skating in Rockefeller Center. It appeared in *Newsday* and, as usual, I was being the trend setter. I wore an evening suit with a white turtle neck. Such high fashion, and such a clown.

No matter what kind of good things were going on in my worlds of work and friends during the '70s, I had terrible sadness, too. First, there was Mother's illness, then there was her death and dealing with it. Mother's conditioned had worsened in 1973, and I made frequent trips to Raleigh to be with her. Things were always the same between the two of us, despite her physical deterioration, but then there came a time when that changed. I went into her hospital room to say that I was leaving to go back to New York. She said, "Son I think you're being selfish."

I got very defensive and thought, "What a terrible thing that is to say to me."

She continued, "I know you love to be with me, but if you are praying I'll be here the next time you can get away to visit me, that's selfish. If you are praying I get well, or that I rest in peace, then you are thinking of me, not yourself. Randy, living in my condition is not living at all."

Mother was the only person who knew just how much I enjoyed her company. She was just crazy about me and it made me feel like I could accomplish anything. She showed this in so many ways. We were very close friends. I wondered a billion times afterwards, which did I do? Did I pray that she would be here just because I wanted her to be here, or did she I pray she rest in peace. It's a good and brave thing for parents to ask, "Which are you doing?"

Just before Mother died, she had asked to be buried in a

white casket. She said, "I have lived a good, clean life and I think it would be appropriate. I do not want a brown, black, or steel-grey casket." So, after she died, I had to go out and see if such a thing existed.

Mabel Holland Trull died July 31, 1973. She was only 66 and was survived by her parents. The *News and Observer* noted her 16-year term of service on the Wake County Board of Elections and her 30-year career as a "noted antique collector."

I found only two, chose one, and ordered the casket spray. I was insistent that the florists cover the casket completely with roses. I told them I did not want to see the casket at all, and not to use any ribbons. I ordered deep red roses at the top, then a gradual turning to pale pink roses at the bottom.

Before the funeral, I wrote my own eulogy to her on an index card and delivered it during the service:

"To me, she was so beautiful with her wonderful smile, sparkling eyes, and that true feeling that her beauty came from within!

"To me, she was so strong for all that was good and right, giving strength to others through words and deeds.

"To me, she was brave through all that life had to offer, always keeping her chin high, looking towards the heavens for her strength.

"To me, she was a living example of life with God at your

side, always believing that through prayer you could find your way.

"To others, she was a wonderful wife, a loving grandmother, but to me, most of all, she was my mother and my friend."

My father had a hard time at first, but gradually seemed to dig himself out. In the fall of 1975, his birthday was coming up, and I called to ask Dad if he would like to have a big party and invite all his friends. He said yes, but he just didn't want to spend any money. That was fine, as I wanted to do this for him at my expense. It is hard to remember just where I started with this party, but I am pretty sure it was the invitations.

I sent out about two hundred of these, inviting all for cocktails, dinner and dancing, but the list just kept growing. I lined the driveway with small white bags filled with sand and a candle in each, and it took two hundred bags to light the drive. I hired young men from N.C. State University to park the cars, as we had plenty of space for them, and had them issue tickets to people so that they could find the cars. I also ordered a blooming orchid tree for the living room, and hundreds of white mums for the steps and fireplaces. Four huge palm trees were put in the foyer, but the ceilings in the house were 12'6", so there was no problem about their height.

As the guests entered the house, Dad and I greeted them at the door, and I told them feel free to wander through the house, then go out into the back yard. We had a bar set up in the garage, and I had covered it to look like a hunter-green tent. The front driveway served as the dance floor, the food was under the center tent, and the trees were all back-lit, so it was like eating in a garden. We had a wonderful Dixieland band, and all in all, it was a grand party.

Though amazed, Randy's father grew to fully appreciate his son's artistic success. Randy's Seven Gables Party, given in Monk Trull's honor, was a labor of love. (The *News and Observer*, courtesy of NC Dept. of Cultural Resources)

Some of the ladies walking through the house asked Dad who slept in the front bedroom, which was all done up in white organdy. He just laughed and told them no one — it was just for show. One lady looked at one of the other bedrooms, and said she could not believe it, but the walls matched the bedspread, the sheets, and the towels. In fact, everything in the room was the same pattern as one that I had done for Fieldcrest. I just took the quilted fabric, stretched it on the walls, the towels, even the toilet paper, in that same pattern.

It was not the Raleigh type of party, but I guess that I wanted them to know I knew how to do a party. The newspaper came out, took photos, and ran an article on the event. There was even a picture of Dad and me standing in the living room. It was one of those moments when I think he was proud of me.

It was a little strange after mother passed away, as Dad was living out in that house by himself, and I was living in New York. We set up a code so that I could talk to him in the evening, as he said all the ladies were calling on him,

This photo appeared in a 12-page article House Beautiful ran on Randy's redecoration of Seven Gables entitled "Echoing the Old South."

echoing the old south

so if he did not speak to them during the day, he would not answer the phone at night. We talked frequently, and one day he said he was thinking about getting a new car. I told him that I would give him one if he would just tell me what he wanted, and what color. He decided that he wanted a Cadillac Fleetwood, and he wanted a diesel. I told him he was not going to save any money as he would not burn enough to pay for the diesel car, but that is what he wanted, so that is what I got him.

I ordered it in New York, and then drove it down to Raleigh. He really thought he was happy man when he got it. About three weeks later, I was talking to my sister-in-law Nita and I asked where Dad was. She said I don't think you are going to be too happy with him when you find out what he has done. There was this big pause on the telephone, and she took a big breath and said, "I think he is out trading that car that you gave him." I went quite mad, but since she had told me, I could not say anything until my father told me himself.

I was really ready for him that evening when I called, and said, "Well, how was your day?"

At that, his voice changed, and he asked if I had been talking to Nita. I told him I had, and then asked what was wrong with the car that I gave him. He said, "Well, it did not have a thermometer on the outside mirror, and I liked the way the trunk looked on this new model, since it was more like an older car." Sometimes you cannot win for trying.

Sometime in 1974, I decided to restore the house in Raleigh, as I thought it would be a great place to give to the state as a historical landmark. It was the last grand old farmhouse and it had belonged to Mr. Lynn, so it became a project when my father said he was not going to spend a dime on that house. If I wanted it, I could have it to do whatever I wanted to. It was another project, and I started it with much excitement.

I had a cement driveway put in that was the length of a runway at the airport. I also found a chandelier that mother and I had bought years ago, and I started taking it to New York in pieces, not even sure what it would look like when I got it put together. I gave it to Albert Nestle who was the best at fixing this sort of thing, and when he had it together, he offered to buy it from me. It was a six-foot-tall Waterford, and truly beautiful. I said I would never have been able to afford one like this if I'd bought it outright, and that I was going to ship it to home to Raleigh.

I had a good friend who carried truckloads of quilted fiber from Brooklyn to North Carolina, and I asked him if he could just sit it in the truck with all the fiber and bring it to the house in Raleigh. I am quite the talker, and I convinced him. They packed it in twelve-square-foot crate, and hung it inside. Then they blew all those little Styrofoam balls inside so that it would not move. This all seemed really easy to me.

When it arrived, my friend Buddy got to Raleigh and called my father. He told him he had a crate to bring out to the house. I didn't think much about it, but when they set the crate in the front yard (which is full of huge old oak trees) and started to open it, the wind blew those thousands of Styrofoam balls all over the yard. They stuck all in the trees and it looked like it had snowed.

Buddy called and told me that I should not rush home, as Dad was really boiling mad at me. He thought they would never be able to get those balls out of the yard, and on top of that, the chandelier weighed three hundred pounds. Before they could mount it, they would have to add some support in the ceiling. After all those years, it seemed that Dad would be used to dealing with my mad ideas, but he wasn't. I waited a few days, then called and asked. "Isn't it beautiful?" I can't write what he said, but he got over it.

My father had remarried, and Eloise was really good for Dad, but not so easy for me as she had her plans for what they would do, and where they would live. She had a house on Carolina Beach, and one in Saint Croix, and she thought that shuttling back-and-forth was a perfect way to live. The house on the island, however, was becoming more dangerous, and they both were concerned.

She finally decided to sell the St. Croix house, but was not going to leave until it was sold, as she thought the locals would wreck it. Dad and Eloise stayed there for almost a year, then they moved back to Carolina Beach and stayed there. They went up to Raleigh when there was a party, or one of them had to go to the doctor. Neither of them believed in the doctors in Wilmington.

Eloise had a daughter who lived in Miami. When Dad and Eloise decided to get married, they planned the wedding for the summer, and had it at Carolina Beach, but the daughter did not attend. She didn't even send a note or call—nothing. It was like she did not know, or care about, Eloise. I never understood that.

It was a hot summer day for the wedding, and after the wedding I went out on the beach to swim and try to cool off. Looking back at the house, I saw my father packing his car, and walked up to ask him what he was doing. He said they were going on their honeymoon. I reminded him that this was their house, and told him the rest of us would leave.

He laughed, and kept packing. As we all stood out on

Randy's stepmother, Eloise Jones Dixon, was a native of Laurinburg, NC.
"She was good looking and a great dresser, too. Although he was up in
years when they married, he lived another seven."

the street, we threw rice at their car, and they drove off.
About an hour later, he called and said that they were at
Wrightsville Beach, at the Blockade Runner, and for us
to come over and have dinner. We did this, then all went
dancing, as he and Eloise loved to dance. Since Wrightsville
Beach is only twelve miles from Carolina Beach, this seemed
almost funny, but we all had fun. It wasn't much of a trip for
them, but it was their choice.

There was so much going on in the '70s, I just flowed
with the wind and kept moving along. I filled my life with
more ideas and projects that sometimes I wondered what
happened to those years: they just flew by! Looking back at
that decade, I guess the most historic social event for me was

being invited to the opening of the famous, and infamous, Studio 54 in New York. That was in 1977, and I had just met a really great gal named Sarah who was from England. We had become great friends so I took her as my date that night. Dressed to perfection, we arrived in a Rolls-Royce, along with some of our other friends. Though it was exciting to be there, Studio 54 was a mad house. It was so loud and crazy that you could hardly hear your own voice. Sarah and I left and went back to someone's apartment where we drank champagne and had our own little party.

7 | *Dealing with the Eighties*

THE '80S WERE A NEW TIME, a new place, and there was a new twist in my career as I was heading out there on my own. Since I was doing my own thing, and with no big company to back me up, it made me think a lot more about costs. I'm not sure that I really knew just what I was doing, but I had a good reputation, and many things that I hoped for had worked out, so I opened my own office.

The tenth floor location at 267 Fifth Avenue was a wonderful space, and had a corner office with twelve-foot ceilings and three large windows. The office was fixed to the nines, with gray moiré draperies at the windows, and gray carpeting. My desk was a beautiful nineteenth century Louis XVI, and the conference table was finished to look like Lapis Lazuli, with six arm chairs done in dark blue to match. I also had a great-looking chandelier hanging over the table. I wanted people to think that I looked really successful when they came into my office, so I focused on its appearance to give that impression. I also wanted them to think that I was something special, even if it was a bit of a lie. But who cared? It worked for me!

Jeff Thompson was the one who told me to go out on my own to begin with, so it seemed almost appropriate that he gave me the office window treatments, and a new client from Canada to help me set up and get things started.

It seems funny to say "get started" when you realize I was already fifty years old, but opening this grand office and doing it on my own was not an easy thing. Let's face it: I have always loved a challenge, and man, this was going to be a big one.

Within a month I had four or five accounts, and was calling on contacts that I had. One of those was Dave Talbert, who was at Cameo Curtain Company. At one point in his career, he had been at Croscill, and he knew what I did for them. He was thrilled that I had left there. Now he could try to move in to that market, as Croscill was his competition. He wanted me to do things for his outfit, so it worked out great for us both. I later learned from Dave that he called Mike up at Croscill and said, "You are mad to let him go. Now I will get some of those winner clients with Randy." As it turned out he was right.

I created a whole new look for Cameo in satin and lace, and one day the buyer from Spiegel was in the showroom. I started talking to him about this item, and since it was late in the day, and Dave thought no one was going to be industrious, he had left me alone in the showroom.

When Dave came to the office the next day, I told him that the fellow had placed an order. He looked shocked, but was delighted. The item I designed eventually turned out to be their biggest seller, and even the buyer from Spiegel got promoted due to its success. David made money, and both my ego and pocketbook fattened along with his.

One day, while I was in the showroom, someone asked

me how old I was. I thought that it was rude of them to ask me, but I said that I was somewhere between twenty-nine and death. A listener commented that the line had come from Auntie Mame, and was actually "somewhere between thirty-nine and death."

My answer to that was to say, "I just wanted to give them more room to negotiate." With that, everyone broke up laughing!

I was lucky enough to work with lots of fun people during this time. One evening, as I was heading home, an office assistant said that she needed a taxi home, and asked if we could share one since we both lived uptown. She said she would drop me off on 57th Street, where I lived at that time. When we got in the cab, we started chatting, then suddenly we were on my corner. I jumped out of the cab, stuck my head back in, and said, "You were a lot of fun, Honey. I will call you again when I am in town." Then I slammed the door and off she went in the cab.

The next day, she told me she could have killed me, as the cab driver turned to her and said, "I'll turn off the meter, drive you home, and come up and spend some time with you if you like." This was not too surprising considering the fact that she was so beautiful, but there she sat, trapped in the back of the cab, and ready to shoot me. She managed to keep her cool, give the guy some quick retort to diffuse the situation, and get out of there.

About this time, someone from Montgomery Ward came to me and asked if I would be willing for them to use my name, and then put together a whole section in their catalog. To tell the truth it, was a big break for me as the project ended up being twelve pages of print in home furnishings. I did very well with this program, and the companies that made the products were also very happy. It was a big hit at the time, but I could see that this company was not going anywhere, so I did not try to push hard to stay with them.

I also spent time in Chicago, at their home office, and thought, this is a company headed to nowhere fast. It was like a big ark, and everyone was just living off the past triumphs, but they were not even thinking about the future. On one of these visits, I talked to the table buyer about buying cloth from Europe, but he said that they did not buy cloth from overseas manufacturers. That sounded fine, but the next time I was out in Chicago, I asked where the buyer of tablecloths was, and they said he was on a trip around the world. This made no sense to me, considering our last conversation, but maybe he had listened to me anyway, and was looking around at possibilities.

Life does not always go the way you want it to go. The head of that division left, and the new guy in charge did not like me. At that point, I was doing very well in my business, so I was not going to let him ruin my fun.

At one of the industry parties that I attended, one of the new upper-level managers from Ward was there. When the party was over, I offered to give him and his wife a lift to their hotel. I was doing very well, and had sold some real-estate recently, so I had a custom Lincoln made for me, and kept it and a driver handy for times like this.

As we headed for his hotel, this fellow was gauche enough to ask if this was that my car and driver, then acted like it was a sin for me to have it. I politely told him that if he thought my working for Montgomery Ward would keep me poor, then he made a big mistake. I would have this car and driver with or without them. He never got over that, but too bad. It was not long after that evening he canceled my agreement, which really had no effect on me, as I thought they were headed down the tube. I guess it turned out that I was right.

I was able to hire a friend, Dorothy Steelman, to work in the design department that I set up, and the two of us started the show trying to look like we really knew just what we were doing. Dorothy was an old friend of mine who had worked at Kandell in the design department, and when she got married, she stayed home to raise the kids. Now that they were grown, and her marriage was not going all that well, she wanted to show everyone that she could make it on her own. Believe me, she had what it takes to stand up and say, "Watch me!" Both of us were doing things we never even thought of doing, but time shows you that many things are possible, and that you can have fun if you love what you do. Now all we needed were some clients, and I went out to dig them up.

While I was gone, some came into the office on their own, as they knew what I had done for other outfits in the past, and they wanted me to do special things for them, too. Sears of Canada wanted some products made for their bed linen department, and over the years I had was able to get between eight and ten pages in the catalog they sent out. That turned out to be a great beginning.

Dave was the president of Cameo, and wanted me to work for his firm, as well. I did not know all that went on behind the scenes in the business, but he had worked at Croscill before me and knew Mike Kahn very well. Although Dave had originally called Mike and told him that he was crazy to let me leave, he was glad now, since I could now do things for him. What a joke this was to me, as I never knew what had happened until many years later, when Dave told me the story.

Designs

Whether pulling bedspread and tablecloth designs from his rich imagination, or redecorating a favorite space like Seven Gables, Randy has the ability to create products that sell and interiors that please family, friends, clients, and the media.

Lynville
for Kemp & Beatle

Dave was very tall, good-looking, and a really easy person to work for, so that made the job easy. At one meeting in his showroom, the Spiegel's catalog buyer was there and I was showing him what I thought was as great idea. Dave just stood there, and as it was late in the evening, he excused himself and left.

The next morning I told Dave that Spiegel's had bought my new program just the way I designed it, and he was shocked, but delighted. It turned out to be the biggest thing they had, and the buyer became a hero, and even got a promotion. Dave realized he had, in me, one of those Croscill winners he wanted. I made enough money from my working relationship with him that I was able to keep my private office and company going.

Amusing things happen to a nut like me. Sometimes I would just charge into the office at Cameo, all tuned up, thinking about my new ideas, but not really thinking about the other people who might be there. Everyone was busy, but whatever I had on my mind was the most important thing for Dave to hear—and right then.

One afternoon, Dave was sitting in the showroom, and I came charging in. I walked over to where he was sitting with some customers, and barged right into the conversation. These guys were from someplace like Kansas, and were real square, so dealing with someone like me was a real change for them.

I leaned over to Dave and said, "Excuse me, but could you tell me when is the breakfast tomorrow morning, and where it is?"

He just leaned back in his chair and said, "At the Prince George Hotel, at eight in the morning. What do you think I should wear?"

To this, I immediately blurted, "Oh I don't know—just wear a string of pearls and a fur coat."

With that, he broke up laughing, but the people from Kansas just looked at each other and must have thought to themselves, what a weird outfit. To tell the truth, I had heard it in some old Bette Davis movie I think, but just remembering lines like that sometimes can help get a laugh out of people.

Another time, Dave and I took some customers out to lunch. As we walked along the street, he hit an uneven piece of sidewalk. I just looked over, smiled, and said to the customer, "He's just not use to wearing flats," and they all broke up laughing. At least that group had a sense of humor. You just never know what I might say—I certainly don't.

In the fall of 1982, an upper-level manager from Montgomery Ward arrived at my office and said the company would like for me to build a major product program for them. It was a great chance, and challenge, for me. I thought it could be a really big deal, and I told them that I would want a fifty-thousand-dollar deposit check up front. They wrote me the check, and it was off to the next challenge for Randy. By this point, there was so much work going on in the office, I hired another woman to work in the art department, and a man to help with all the other things that were going on. I also hired a secretary to take care of the books, and try to keep things straight as I could make a real mess in about one minute.

Julie was good, but she was a really nice girl from Brooklyn who had not dealt with the mad world of designers, or someone like me. She took it all in her stride, however. I must say that through all these changes, Dorothy never lost her cool. She could deal with all my madness, even if she wondered where it all came from, but it worked out. She was great, and boy, did we stay busy.

Every morning, when I would look out from my kitchen apartment window on 57th Street, there was this pleasant woman across from me, there in the next building. I would smile and wave, and one day we began to talk back and forth across the space between the buildings. Later, she opened the window and invited me to come to a cocktail party. It turns out that she was Princess Donatella Colonna Fiorenzi dei Conti di Montecerno, a real grand lady, and we have been friends for twenty years.

When I went to Princess Donatella's party, I saw a really lovely woman, but I did not know who she was. Some guy at that party seemed to be really working her over, and trying to let her know he was really some great person. I stepped in to try to make it more pleasant for her, with only politeness and no pressure from me. Since that evening, Rosita Fanto and I have been great friends.

Rosita is multilingual, multicultural, multi-exiled, and multi-assimilated. She has lived in many places, including Romania, Brazil, the United States, Switzerland, Italy, England, France, and Monaco. She is a teacher, author, artist, and film producer. Her credits range from work on a documentary about sculptor Henry Moore for French television, to *Presage*, a visual and tactile publication that grew to three hundred volumes and is exhibited in major museums worldwide. Rosita has been the originator of countless unusual and offbeat ventures such a collaboration with Richard Ellman to create the "Oscar Wilde Playing Cards."

So, I think to myself, "Why in the world did she ever waste her time hanging out with me?" She did, though—and we still see one another several times a year. To tell the truth, I should have asked her to marry me, and I think we would have had a great life together. She came from another world, however, and I was just not in that league. I have been the lucky one, as she has put up with me for all these years, and made me feel like someone special.

Rosita has lived in Monaco for years, and she still does. In her heyday, the *New York Times* once called her, the "Brazilian Bombshell." I had an opportunity to meet her during this difficult time, but I declined out of respect for the situation. She has even written a few books of her own. I suspect one would not guess her wealth apart from her surroundings. There are many people in the world who flaunt their wealth, but I believe that it is safe to say that she is not one of them.

Randy and Rosita Fanto of Monte Carlo became the best of friends after being introduced by Princess Donatella in the 1980s. 30 years later, they stay connected by phone and visits.

Rosita invited me to visit her in Monte Carlo, and I said yes in a heartbeat. As I planned for the trip, I was really excited, but tried to calm down as I got ready. On one of those days just before I left, I was out of the office, and Rosita called. When I got back, Julie looked at me and said, "Mr. Trull, Miss Fanto called from Monte Carlo, and said you should bring your evening clothes, as you will be entertained."

I thanked Julie, and went on about my day. Two or three days later, I came back to the office from a meeting, and Julie had this funny look on her face. She said, "Mr. Trull, Rosita Fanto called again from Monte Carlo, and said she would like to know what you want to have for breakfast."

I smiled and said, "Tell her fresh orange juice and a croissant."

She just looked at me and said, "Yes, Mr. Trull!"

Well, heaven help us, because a few days after this, I

 walked back into the office after lunch and I could see Julie was really bent out of shape. She said that Miss Fanto had called from Monte Carlo again, and said that the traffic from the Nice airport to Monte Carlo was terrible, so she would arrange for a helicopter to take me to her. With all this, Julie looked at me like who were we kidding, and said, "Who is this broad, anyway?"

Randy keeps a hand on his Louis XVI desk while posing in his office, about 1973. "I became known for that hankerchief. I always had a silk one. I didn't wear casual clothes again until I returned to the South," he said in 2009.

The '80s were a strange time for me, as I was making good money, and was trying to build a strong base from my accounts. Since I was making enough money, life was easier for me, and things just seem to be heading where I needed them to. Offers for work came along consistently enough that I really did not need to go looking for customers, so I tried to sit back a little and just have fun. I worked as hard as I needed to, and I loved what I was doing. The thought of stopping just did not enter my head.

I made another interesting contact early on, a man named Norman

In addition to Yves St. Laurent and Collier Campbell, Randy was also featured alongside Geoffrey Beeene, Pierre Cardin, and Cathy Hardwick in the June 7, 1982 issue of *Retailing Home Furnishings.*

Alexander, who lives in his own building in New York City and made his fortune inventing and selling polyester fabric. On each floor of his five-story home, there is approximately $100 million in fine art. He has nine masks made by Pablo Picasso, and this is just the tip of the iceberg. I became friends with him as we worked together to build a textile mill in North Carolina, and we both became friends of Princess Donatella Colonna.

For a while there seemed to be no end to his wealth. Jokingly, he once told a friend, "I think I'll give Randy a 'Share the Wealth Card' from the game, Life, for his birthday." However, while in his employ, I met people whose fortunes dwarfed his by comparison. So it began years ago, with me as a naïve, young college student fresh out of college, and he, a wealthy and successful designer, who was determined to teach this kid about the realities of life.

Luther Travis was one of the best designers I had ever known and his talent seemed unlimited. Luther was retired from Bloomcraft where he had worked for twenty-eight years. He contacted me and asked if I might like to take him on as a partner. It was an honor for me, because Luther was one of the best print designers in the world. He had a great deal to do with Bloomcraft's success in the fabric business and his talent kept them as a leader during his stay there. We changed the name Randy Trull Designs to Trull-Travis Designs, and went right to work. The change gave me a new road and a new challenge.

Luther and I were a strange mix, because he was and is a very private person and doesn't blow his own horn. He just does his creative thing quietly and lets it move out into the market and work for the good of the company he works for. So each of us had to think about how to work with the other and just what it would take to make our company profitable. Obviously, I was and still am a talker and salesmen. Since Luther was just the opposite, we would discuss each project, then develop a plan for my presentation to the customer.

I grasped the fact quickly that Luther did not like to be cruised about his designs, so I learned to just walk into his office and say something like, "That design is just beautiful, but I think if you just would make a few changes it would be a real winner." Dorothy would just break up laughing because she knew I was always going to say the same sort of thing to him; a few buttery words followed by some sort of criticism. Usually, Luther would just look at me, then change the design an hour or two later.

That repeating rhythm in our working relationship was effective, and we were a hit in the market place, but, personally, we never were close friends. We put up with each other and I am sure he had a harder time putting up with my madness than I ever had working with him. It was one of those bonds that made us successful, but never close.

By the late '80s, I was really enjoying the fruits of my success. I traveled at will and allowed myself some luxuries I could not have afforded when I was younger. As I became better known, invitations to really nice cocktail parties came along much more frequently, and that always gave me a rush. I always seemed to be on the fringe of high society. Meeting fun people who probably would not remember my name gave me an opportunity to say just about anything that came to mind. My mouth has always evidenced my madness.

Milton Goldman, the famous theatrical agent, gave very nice parties and he introduced me to Christopher Plummer at one them. He was playing the role of Daddy Warbucks in the Broadway version of *Annie* at that time and his head was shaved for the part. I just looked at him, shook his hand, and said, "You must tell me who your hair dresser is as I want to be sure to skip him."

Plummer broke up laughing and said, "Good line, fellow."

Just as I am usually quick to speak, my friend Sybil Connolly exhibited the dignity of silence. Sybil and I got along well. She was the famous Irish courtier and was known for her fine tweed designs. She brought an Irish accent to much of her design work and I guess the most famous example of that was the dress she designed for Jackie Kennedy's official portrait.

I was introduced to Sybil as "Randy Trull." Immediately, she asked me what my Christian name was. I answered, Randolph Holland Trull. She answered, "Then, I shall call you Randolph." She did call me Randolph, always. She kept the reason silent, but I knew it was because, in the UK, the word randy is a slang expression used to describe someone who has hot pants.

I went to Ireland to visit Sybil while we were working on a project together. Her chauffeur picked me up at the airport and as we were riding through the countryside, I made the big mistake of saying how little I knew about the Irish trauma. He replied that 750 years ago the English sent all their bad people to Ireland and I started thinking, "How far could Sybil live from the airport?"

When we got close to Sybil's house, I said, "Well, just what do think the solution would be?"

He just looked at me and said, "We just need to send all those bad people back. I thought that after 750 years, that would be quite a job.

I entered the house where there was a maid and what looked like a butler. The maid said that I would be staying out in the yard in the guest cottage. It turned out to be the most beautiful cottage you can imagine. She told me to go upstairs and pick my room, since I was the only guest at that time, so I picked what I thought was the most fabulous room. The maid had my clothes pressed and laid them out for the evening.

I joined Sybil downstairs for tea at three o'clock. When she entered the room and greeted me, she asked how long I would be staying. I looked at her and said, "Oh, about a month. Who in their right mind would want to hurry?"

She looked a little shocked, but stayed calm.

I just laughed and said, "No, I am just staying a couple of days."

Back in New York, I took Sybil to an elegant party one night, and while we were returning to her apartment in the taxi she started telling me about something she had experienced earlier that day. She said she was riding in a taxi and told the driver to please drive more slowly since she was a foreigner and New York style driving frightened her. He replied, "You sound just like my mother." Then, when she got out of the taxi, the driver looked at her with her peaches and cream completion and with hair tainted blue and said, "You even look like my mother." This wouldn't have been so amazing except for the fact that the taxi driver was black. I broke up laughing but Sybil just sat there demurely like a proper women who was charming, but somewhat in another world.

One day in 1988, I was having a very bad day. Nothing seemed to be working right. Suddenly, my secretary came into my office and said that there was a Mr. Golble from Glen Raven Mills outside who would like to talk with me. I figured this man would be just another $1500-a-year account because I had never heard of him before. I told her to send him in and I would get rid of him in a hurry.

He was very nice and said that they would be interested in hiring me to be a consultant to Sunbrella which belongs to Glen Raven Mills. Sunbrella is a sturdy, colorful, fade-resistant fabric that is the standard for boats and fine outdoor furnishings, but I didn't know a thing about it at the time. So, I said to him, "You must understand that I don't take a account unless it can produce at least $50,000 a year."

He just looked at me and said," I don't think that is a problem."

Well, that took me back. I asked him how much business the company did and he said it was privately owned and that they did not publish figures, but that the total was in excess of $200 million. I thought to myself, "Kill yourself, Trull. You could have said a $100 thousand." Unfortunately, they never forgot the number I quoted. They always just said, "You should be happy with what you're getting." And, to tell the truth, I was.

Let's face it: I do like a challenge, and going to work for Glen Raven Mills gave me a chance to do something different. The casual furniture industry was a whole new world of work for me, but I jumped in like a mad man. From the start, I was consumed with designing Sunbrella fabrics, because of the material's fine qualities and natural dyes. It makes me feel good now to know that my artistic creations are sitting out there on porches and decks across the country, and that the owners are so pleased.

I have been working for Glen Raven Mills for twenty-five years now. I'm glad I could make the transition from one industry to another. It kept me fresh. I'm almost eighty years old, and I still love going to work and enjoy thinking up designs and new ways to use the products.

At Glen Raven, I was a new face with new ideas for them. The mix seemed to work for both of us. It was another new world, and I approached it in my usual gung ho way. I did not think about where it would lead. I just went forward to meet a new challenge for Randy. Before, I had become a personality and an authority in the house interiors industry. I dove right into a whole new design field. Now, twenty years later, I am still creating Sunbrella designs for Glen Raven. I have met the challenges of the house interiors industry and the casual furniture industry, and I feel that I've conquered both.

When I began working with Sunbrella, I listened to everything my bosses thought would be good for the company, and then I just brushed it off. I thought, "Oh well, I will think about that later." Then I just charged ahead trying to come up with new design ideas and new things to do with Sunbrella. Even though I did take the company forward, I must admit I caused anguish to those who had to work in the office. I stirred up the pot on a regular basis. Sometimes when I walked into Glen Raven offices it looked like they all took a deep breath, for they had no idea what I was up to. They would get one pot settled, then I'd walk in and stir up another.

When I first started working with Glen Raven they only worked in solids, stripes, and a few checks. That left the field wide open for me to dream up more styles. The folks at Glen Raven wanted to do prints and that was easy for me. As soon as I had some designs to show, I hit the road to show it to their customers. The prints really did do well, but I knew there was a lot more that could be done.

I remembered Sunbury Mills, a Jacquard mill that made great things. I thought, "Why not do Jacquards in Sunbrella?" So I called my friend at Sunbury, Mark Grigalunas, who was head of the design group there and who I thought was the best there was in Jacquards. I told him what I wanted to do and he went all out to make it happen. I think few people saw what Mark and I saw, or knew we could make it work.

When we showed the designs to some of the people at Glen Raven they just said they were too expensive and that no one would buy them. Well, Big Mouth Trull said, "Just grant me a royalty and if I sell some I will make money."

They just said, "Okay, smart ass. Go for it."

Mark was like a rock, backing me and leading me. We went to Kravet Fabrics and showed them a program and they bought the whole thing. When I called Glen Raven and told them I had an order, they just scoffed and said, "Well, how much is the order?"

I laughed and said, "Oh, $556,000 dollars, and this is just the opening order."

"I told people this is the Greek cook I keep on my boat, but he's actually Mark Grigalunas, Executive Vice President of Sunbury Mills. He just loved to cook," said Randy.

From then on, Jacquards became a part of Sunbrella. I hit the road and sold them just every place I could. Sunbury jumped on this like a fly sticking to tar paper, and Sunbrella and Sunbury were off then on a new road. That process has now changed the road and has been great for companies and the industry as a whole.

Age does make one think that you should slow down some, but loving the work makes me want to keep going. It is fun to think out of the box in unusual creative ways that surprise the mathematical geniuses in a company. I enjoy doing things that say, "Gotcha!"

Making trim and cords to use with Sunbrella seemed like a great idea, so I was off in a new direction, designing trimmings to use with the fabric. I had a new idea and a new product and I was rushing around the marketplace trying to get people to like it and use it. After three or four years, people decided that it was a good idea, so now there was another successful Sunbrella product in the market place.

Recently, I thought, "Gosh, why not try to do another silk idea, because silk is in again." We did not have that many shiny yarns to choose from, so I thought, "Okay, let's do a raw silk look." From that came the pattern Dupioni and it has turned out to be a big hit for Sunbrella.

In the world of fabric design, we don't live in a revolution. We live in an evolution. This old guy remembers what worked before and I keep bringing things back in a new way for a new generation of buyers. I told you I was lucky, and I am, but just the process of remembering has helped make me even luckier.

8 | *Older and Wiser in the Nineties*

THE '90S WERE VERY DIFFERENT for me, as I was growing older. Luther Travis and I had gone our separate ways, and now I was back to operating as Randy Trull. I moved my office into the twenty-first floor of 261 Fifth Avenue. It was a great space, and things were going well for me since I had several artists working in the studio, and had a really great helper in Julie. She really wanted to become a designer, so she was forever coming into the studio and giving her opinion on things. That was not all bad, but she did not like to be told that an idea she had was not right for me or the line. We all have to learn things, and I must say she did study how we did things, and learned a lot that helped her after she left me.

In October of 1990, the Curtain and Domestic Industry honored me as one the designers of the year. They said I had made a great noise and had made things happen, and thanked me for stepping up to the plate, coming out of the back room where most designers were hidden, talking directly to customers, and helping customers see what was good and new in the market.

Pictured at the podium are Ciro "Chip" Scala, Randy, and Edith Hecht.

I found myself up on the stage with Martha Stewart, Mary Stevens (of Waverly Fabrics), and Raymond Waites. There were over five hundred people sitting there, all dressed up, hoping the talks would be short and then we could all have dinner. Well, some of the people who spoke thanked everyone in their entire family, and talked for way too long, even though the presenters had asked us not to talk over five minutes. The plan was that they were to give you the award, and then you were to follow with your short, "Thank you."

Since I was able to choose the people to give me my award, I had Chip Scala and Edith Hecht give me mine. Chip spoke first, and when he got up there, he said "What can I say about Randy Trull that he has not already said about himself?" With that, the place broke up laughing.

After Edith made some remarks, it was my turn. I went on to say that a lot of the people there had started at the same time I did, and now some of their children were in the business. When I first came into the business, I got married to an industry. I then thanked them from the bottom of my heart for making it a wonderful evening for me.

The talk took less than two minutes, and the applause was incredible. After that, a friend came up to me and said, "What a great speech!" I responded, "What a liar you are." It was short, and everyone was so glad. Another friend walked over to ask if my feelings were hurt from what Chip had said, and I laughed. I said, "Why not at all. He was telling the truth. I had to go out and plug for myself, as I had no large company there to promote me. Just me, my little office, and my big mouth. Ha, ha, ha!"

I began to think that it was time to slow down, and to travel some, maybe even think about retiring, as I was sixty years old. The young crowd coming along made it harder to spend the time, as they were always saying, "Hire me to design something for you." I wanted to continue doing my own thing, so I spent lots of time trying to find new looks and working on new ideas. I was traveling all over the world.

I had done a lot of work with Ludvig Svensson from Sweden, and had become close to the Ludvigsons who owned the company. They just treated me like part of their wonderful family. It is strange how that can happen sometimes. I have such feeling for them and they always are so warm and friendly to me. Meeting them was a really lucky break for me. I felt at home from the first day, when they invited me to dinner at their home.

They had venison—deer meat—which to Sweden is like chicken to the American South. I wanted to be a good guest, but all I could think of Rudolf the Red-Nosed Reindeer. I felt almost like a cannibal eating it, but, to my surprise, I really liked it. So, the good old Southern boy added another food to his "favorites" list, and became a little more worldly.

About this time, I started to represent them in the U.S. since I knew most of the people in the industry. It was more fun than work, except when I had to travel with Ivan the boss. He was a mad man to travel with, and he had ex-tremely heavy bags, filled with samples. To tell the truth, I could hardly lift those bags.

Ivan would race from city to city, all over the country and Canada. That was a little

"That's Magdalena Ludvigson," said Randy. "Beautiful and smart, she is now married and has three sons."

much for me and those damned bags. I would tell Ivan that a customer we were headed to did not like the laces, but he was going to show them everything anyway. If they did not like them, no matter what, they were going to see them, and that was that. If they made him an offer for something, he would sit there with his calculator—he just had to have an order. Oh well, it was his company, and I was just there to carry those stupid bags filled with stuff most people did not want to see.

Every year in January, we would go to Frankfurt, Germany to attend a show called "Heimtextil." I learned to really hate that town, as it was damned cold, and it seemed to snow all the time. We got up before daylight, headed to the fair, and stayed indoors until after dark. Each day, I

Ivan, Ann, and Clay Ludvigson pose at their home in Sweden.

headed back to the hotel in darkness, and snow or rain, or a little of both. One year, the rains were so bad that the river that flows through the city flooded the ground floor of our hotel, so we had to wade through water just to get out into the rainy street. What a nightmare that was, and it went on for almost twenty years. Every time, we spent most of the time saying "Hello" and "Glad to see you!" when all you really wanted to do was leave that place.

On one of those trips, the big boss of Glen Raven joined me, and I felt it was my job to be sure he met people, and that we would get to talk to the head of Covington Fabrics. This was a new, and very good, customer of ours. I went by early, made sure the president was there, and told her that we would come by, as the president wanted to say a personal thank you for their business. In truth, I must say that I thought she was a friend. I also felt I had put the two companies together and that things were going well.

When we approached her booth, I thanked her for taking the time to speak to us. The boss from Glen Raven thanked her for doing such a good job with the fabrics, and that he was really pleased at what I done for this project. To everyone's shock, she said she was sorry to hear that.

We stood there for a moment trying to think what to say. I can tell you now I had some really ugly thoughts about what to say, but unlike my usual self, I kept my cool until we walked away. Then I began to fume, thinking how in the world she could have said that about me. To tell the truth, I don't think I ever got over that, but life goes on. I waited, but you can be sure I had my day later!

I was a very visible person in that environment, had been there for years, and knew a fair amount of the crowd. The boss was really nice to me, seemed pleased, and I tried to be sure he saw and met lots of people. When I got home, I heard from the head office that he was worn out from that trip, and that he would not be going back. I knew most of the people at that fair, and he had met them all.

I finally closed my office in New York in 1992, and worked for Holloman Industries in Holly Springs. I sold my company in about 1994, but I still do some consulting work for Glen Raven.

When 1995 rolled around, I was living in Wilmington, North Carolina, while occasionally flying to New York, or dashing over to London, for some fun and wonderful theatre. I received an invitation to a birthday party that was being held in St. Petersburg, Russia, and thought that would be a great trip, as I had not been to Russia. I am not sure that I had any idea what I was doing, but something new and different was up my alley, so I accepted the invitation as soon as I got the full details.

It was Pierre Fredrick Vasserot Merle's sixtieth birthday, and he had decided to have the party in St. Petersburg. It would last five days, since anyone going would want to see some of Russia after travelling that far. I had only one friend that was going, so he would be my only contact besides the host.

Our host told everyone that they could fly on a special flight from New York to St. Petersburg, but I really didn't think much of the airline. I planned my own flight with KLM from Amsterdam to St. Petersburg as I felt safe on that airline. I packed some toilet paper and soap, as I felt sure they would not have these. A friend of mine went there years before and told me that they had terrible paper in the bathrooms. Of course, I didn't really think about it very much or I would have realized that he had gone twenty years before me, and things were vastly changed.

I arrived safely in St. Petersburg, and as I walked toward the customs people, a very large gentleman walked up to me and asked if I was Mr. Trull. I thought they must think I was a gangster or something, since he asked for my passport and my luggage ticket. I wondered—in my nervousness— if should holler out, or just go along calmly. He pointed to a gate, told me to walk through it, and said that he would bring my luggage and take care of my passport. I'm not sure what I thought was going on, but I did what he said and prayed I would see my luggage and passport again.

He came back to me a little while later and told me to get into a huge Mercedes. He put my luggage in the trunk, gave me my passport and told me he was driving me to the hotel. After a bit, we arrived at a truly grand hotel. When

I got out, the doorman asked if I was there for Mr. Merle's birthday celebration, and I said "Yes." It was then he told me to go to the cocktail lounge where Mr. Merle was greeting everyone.

I walked into the lounge, and one of the wait staffers put a glass of champagne in my hand and offered me some caviar. A few yards away, there stood Pierre, greeting everyone. He turned and welcomed me, then started to introduce me to a young lady standing to his left. As he said, "Sarah, this is —" she cut him off, looked straight at me, and said, "Randy, darling! How nice to see you."

Pierre, looking a bit surprised, asked "You know him?

She said, "Why yes, he took me to the opening of Studio 54 in New York."

I was a little taken back since I had almost forgotten that I went to the opening. As it turned out, she was now married and living in England.

Hardly had that happened, when he turned to his right and a guy named Tom, who had been Bill Blass' assistant said, "Hi Randy." Then the guy next to Tom also said hello, and reminded me that he had worked for my friend Jack Silverman at Ogilvy and Mather. After all this, Pierre looked at me like, "whose party is this anyway?" Pierre finally took a deep breath, laughed, and said something like, "Well, just welcome your own friends, Randy."

I eventually headed up to my room, and nearly went into shock. It was as grand as you could imagine, with everything you could think of. This included fresh flowers, a bottle of Vodka with nice glasses, and the program for what we would all be doing while there, complete with the guest list

We went to a special show of the royal ballet, and since we were all dressed in evening clothes, then were off to another really nice hotel for dinner. One evening, we arrived at the Marble Palace and there were waiters standing on each step holding trays of champagne and hors d'oeuvres, and there was music playing all around. It was like being in fairy land.

Then they announced that dinner was served, and we walked over to a table where you were handed a card with your name and table number on it. We then headed into the grand ballroom and found our tables, and what a table setting it was. There were five glasses for each person to enjoy the water, vodka, white, red, and champagne wines. The service was out of this world. Then came a floor show, and finally people danced until all hours of the morning. What an evening.

The next day, we headed out to Catherine's Palace as our host had arranged two tour busses to move us around, and had provided wonderful guides on each bus. They each told us wonderful stories about how it was before the Great Revolution. Catherine's Palace and the park next to it are nearly unbelievable, but as a designer it was just a dream come true.

When we left the Palace we went to Podvorie, a country inn where they were all set up for our lunch. They had five glasses on the table, and I thought, these people do like to drink. A folk dance show provided the centerpiece of the lunch as we dined.

That evening, we headed to Elgin Palace, a truly Russian setting. We were all dressed up, as were the waiters, who had trays of caviar and champagne. As expected, there was music, but this time, the music was real Russian—heavy and loud. From the cocktails, we moved into the ballroom and found our tables. I did not sit with the same people as before, so I was with a different group every evening. The food was excellent, and then there was a floor show of Russian Cossack-style dancers during dinner. Afterwards, there was dancing and drinking until the wee hours of the morning.

The next day, we were taken to the national art gallery. It was closed to the public just for us to have a private showing, and the head took us on a personal tour. My, did this make us all feel special. From there, we went to the Hermitage, and again it was closed to all but us. Pierre must have had some real connections in St. Petersburg.

The last evening we were there, the Stroganoff Palace was our pleasure palace for the evening, and again, it was super, and planned down to the last detail. This was the 'official' birthday party, and there was a reception in the Hall of Mirrors, with light music and another selection wonderful hors d'oeuvres. Finally, we entered the just-refinished ballroom, and found our seats by opening a Faberge-style egg, and on each of these was the date. Trying to describe all these details and make the event live for you is nearly impossible. It was like entering a dream world, long since passed away. It was certainly a trip I shall long remember.

9 | *Still a Part of it All in the New Century*

ON JULY 7TH, 2000, I turned seventy, so I decided to give myself an enormous birthday party. Some people say that when you give yourself a birthday party, it is just an ego trip or a sign of insecurity, but I did not see it that way. I thought of it as an opportunity to see all the friends whom I had known over the years that were still around. It was also an opportunity for me to say to them, "Come, and let's have a wonderful time. Let's be thankful that we are here, and thank you for being so nice to me over the years." So I planned this enormous birthday party in Wilmington, North Carolina, which has been my home base for many years now.

It was a challenge to plan all of this, not unlike planning a wedding. I started arranging the July event back in February, and ordered tablecloths and napkins from India. I wanted something really very special, and worked with an Indian manufacturer I knew. I told him exactly what I wanted, and how I wanted it, and I wanted a very special look at the country club. I thought I was rather clever for beginning all this in February because I would be able to get all the goods and people organized in plenty of time.

In April, I sent out invitations to about two hundred of my closest friends. I invited a big crowd on a whim, but then responses started coming right back to me, and most accepted my invitation. Some of my them were traveling a very long way just be help me celebrate my birthday. So, now I knew I had to get serious about things and start working faster. The three-day event was fast approaching and I had line up plenty of fun things for everyone to do.

I planned a golf outing for Thursday and a tennis match on Friday. Thank the Lord for my cousin, Paula, for she pitched a huge tent in her back yard and hosted a pig picking Friday night. What a party that was! We ate good old-fashioned Southern food, and the guests who were from "away" hardly had a clue what they were eating. That was all right, though, because alcohol flowed throughout the night and those who were confused about their food soon forgot it.

On Saturday night, I hosted a cocktail dinner and dance at the country club and thanks to all those helping me, the place did come together and it looked wonderful. I taped a dollar under each chair and, after one was seated, I ask them to stand up again. Some smart aleck said, "I guess we have to praise Randy before we can eat."

I just smiled and asked everyone to turn their chairs over, then in my most smart ass voice, I said, "See, if you just get off your backside you can make a buck." They must have liked that, because I checked after the party was over and all the dollar bills were gone except one.

I lined up four people to give short speeches. I thought it would be more interesting if they represented different parts of the world, too. Ann Ludvigson was there from Sweden, Leslie Creasey from England, Chip Scala from New York City, and Tim Stephenson from Raleigh.

Left: Randy's cousins, Douglas Gill and Pat Trull Holliday dance at Cape Fear Country Club during Randy's birthday party, 2000.

Below: Randy poses with Tim Stephenson. "I chose speakers for my party from the different parts of my working world. Tim, a proud son of Benson, represented North Carolina; Chip Scala, New York; Ann Ludvigson, Sweden; and Leslie Creasy, England."

I had written, "No Presents," on the invitation, but Michel Kerr and Mark Girgalunas took it on themselves to make a life decision for me. They decided I needed a dog. At the dinner that evening they presented me with a stuffed Bijon Frise and explained that it was just a replica of the real gift. I thought, "What in the world will I do with one of those?"

Randy introduced his friend Gloria Clark (below) to friend Kenny Sprunt (above) at a party in 1994, and they married a year later. Posing with Kenny is Randy's close cousin, Paula Gill Dayvault, hostess for the party.

Mark said the real dog had been born, but that the owner would not let me have her until she was eleven weeks old, and, then, only if she showed no promise of becoming a championship winner. I thought maybe I would be lucky and the dog would win the Westminster Kennel Club trophy, and I would maintain my single status.

No such luck, though.

"It was a long time between" dogs. Randy has only had two dogs, born 65 years apart. "Pooch" arrived about 1935.

The owner called and said they did not think she would be a champion so I could have her. I said, So, I am getting used merchandise?" She explained that my dog was too small and her nose was not the jet black shade judges prefer.

So, I took the dog, or should I say she took me. They told me to brush her at least once a week and wash her every two weeks. Well, I washed her once and somehow the whole house was got messed up. I was not into that scene at all, so I took her to the beauty parlor every Friday after that. She is made to look great there and is treated like a real princess. I get Fridays off, so we are both happy.

I named her after my mother—Princess Mabel—though I am not sure Mother would have thought much about having a dog named after her. She would approved of the way Princess keeps me running. What the hell: I love her, and for ten years now we have been happy together. She plays the princess, and, I, the pea.

I have been lucky enough to spend many years on this earth so far, and I have lied so many times about my age that I really don't know how old I am sometimes. When I look at the real calendar though, I am reminded that, today, I am seventy-nine years old. My God, that is old, but I feel so much younger, and even act younger still. The reality of it is that I have a great deal of difficulty accepting that I was born in July of 1930. It was not really the greatest time to arrive on this earth, in the middle of the Great Depression. Of course I did not really know, because I was just a little baby.

As you get older, you are not able to adjust well to flying or traveling. Thank heavens that my friend Anne was there to pick me up from the airport in Gothenburg, Sweden when I arrived for one of my trips in 2002. We went over

Randy and his current Princess take a spin, about 2005. (Photo by Steve Dayvault)

to her flat, where I spent the evening, and slept until almost eleven o'clock the next morning. I was totally beat up from such a long trip.

After a good night's sleep, I felt better and took myself out to see some of the sights in Gothenburg during the day because Anne was working. Since she was tied up, I had a free day to go around the town and see all of the things that I had never really seen before. I walked down the streets, looked in all of the museums, and checked out all the boats in the harbor. It was a very pleasant day, and I had a chance to look in some of the shops and see some of the products that were appearing in the Swedish market. Late in the afternoon, I met Anne back at the apartment and we drove to Kinna, where Ivan and Clay Ludvigson, Anne's mother and father, lived.

We had dinner there on Friday night, and when we arrived, there were twelve or thirteen people. Clay had organized dinner for everyone, and had places for everyone to sleep. What a super lady she was to have organized all of this madness and make it seem as though it were easy. I had a wonderful little room with my own television set and my own bathroom, all within what I would call their "compound" in Kinna. I did go to bed reasonably early that evening, after eating, but I was up bright and early on Saturday morning.

That morning, there were lots of things happening, with even more people arriving. In fact, the outside of their house looked almost like a used car lot since there were so many automobiles and so many people arriving. Again, Clay organized breakfast for everyone and by lunchtime, there were twenty people for Saturday lunch. The menu was what I would call little hamburgers, but they were much better than ours in the states. These were little beef patties with a wonderful salad side, and some type of hot potato dish. In this group of guests, I met this perfectly wonderful lady from Paris, whose name was René. She was eighty-four years old, but was such a charming lady that we instantly became good buddies. After getting to know her, I poked fun at her and asked if her that if she was that old, would I have to wheel her around in a wheelchair? She immediately came back at me in jest, so we had a glorious time together.

As an added benefit to the day, the crown princess of Sweden came to visit the Ludvigson's factory, so Ivan and his granddaughter Lisa gave her some roses. As Lisa was only six at the time, this made it a really special event, and since there was some press coverage, there were later pictures in all of the newspapers. More people kept arriving, and that evening they had a cocktail party, and everyone seemed to be having a wonderful time. It is interesting to note that this was of the first times I saw a woman with a pants suit, which I found very different, but all the rest had on beautiful dresses. So few women today wear the type of formal and beautiful dresses I saw then.

I was seated at a table with a charming Swedish lady who was from Kinna, and whose husband was a heart surgeon. He was originally from Sweden, but lived in Cleveland and performed major heart surgery in Ohio. Most of the people at my table spoke English, as do most Swedes, which was good for me. It is almost as though Swedish is a second language and that English is the first.

I had a perfectly wonderful time at the party; everyone was so gracious to me. It was certainly a very special event as far as Ivan and Clay were concerned, and they seemed absolutely thrilled that I was there with them. Sunday was spent recuperating, but again my hostess had nearly thirty people in the house for lunch. It was amazing to me that everything flowed as though it was easy to handle that many people and all that food. Sunday evening, after most of the crowd had left, they opened the presents that they had received. I teased Ivan a bit, and said, "Obviously your friends think that you drink a lot, because sixty percent of what they gave you was either champagne or special wines wrapped in floral arrangements."

On Monday morning, I found myself sitting at the airport in Gothenburg, waiting to fly back to London. That afternoon, I had to meet Leslie for a show where we would look at merchandise, then called Rosita Fanto and arranged for me to visit her. That evening was the memorial service for her daughter, Christine, who died from cancer in 2002. Her funeral was very significant because she was so well-loved, and Rosita had called on me to be with her during her time of grieving. There were hundreds of people in attendance, but I was the only person who seemed to provide her with any real comfort or solace. This illustrates the amount of trust and affection that we both had for each other. It is very special to note here that she was afforded every possibility which wealth could provide, but even great wealth cannot remove cancer or tragedy. Christina had a loving family and was a person of inestimable good character.

Her ancestry afforded her a great deal of wealth, and allowed her to stay virtually anywhere in the world for an undetermined amount of time. She was able to live a lifestyle that is much beyond even the wealthiest of people here in the U.S.

10 | *A Retrospective Viewpoint*

THERE WAS A TIME in my life that I realized the boy from the country had gone to the big city, and would never return. I was not the same kid anymore. Funny how it just kind of dawns on you that you are a different person than you were when you started out. Life has a way of leading you down the path you are supposed to take.

It is undeniable that I have told you too often here that I have always been lucky. It is pretty hard to be humble when your parents have spoiled you all along, and harder still when you have had things go your way in nearly every way, all your life. In a nutshell, that has been me, and generally, still is the way my life is going. Now that I have a bit of time and age under my belt, I do believe that I was lucky in other ways that I never knew about then, but that I can better realize and appreciate now.

Having teachers, friends, business owners and contacts in the design world believe enough in me to have given me chances I got, allowed me to really develop and use my creative talents. I might not have gotten as far as I have if it were not for the chances people took when they supported me or gambled on my ideas, which ultimately worked well. My confidence has been built, over time, due to these individuals and their financial or psychological support. Without these influences, and at least indirect sources of guidance, I doubt my life would have turned out quite as much of a success as it has proven to be so far. Hindsight is always clearer than when you are facing down the event right then. With that in mind, I offer thanks to the many gifted and talented people who helped me along the way.

Now, in 2009 at seventy-nine, I am trying to learn to slow down, take a deep breath, and realize that I am not the same kid that started in this design world in 1954. Life is not over, though, and neither is my work, but I do move more slowly. I enjoy running the shop I own in Wilmington, and still buy much of the merchandise in Europe. It's fun to come home and show people of good taste how these fine pieces will enhance their home.

Knowing me, I might come up with another idea for something new in the world of home furnishings. Who knows? Maybe I will try to write a different sort of book one day, if this one ever gets out there. Those people who knew me can laugh a little and think to themselves, "I knew that mad man!"

Who Needs a Decorator: You do!

Helping people decorate can be challenging. When I work on someone's home, I remind myself that I don't live there. I am merely trying to make it a place that exudes good taste and fine design, yet looks like the homeowner, not me. I want to make improvements, but ones that look and feel as if the client might have thought them up.

One thing I know for sure is that decorators are not like surgeons who could make one little mistake and, oops, they have snipped the wrong thing off. Decorating is a more forgiving field. If you live with something for a while and it just does not feel right, keep working with your decorator until you are satisfied with it. If possible, try out new decor on a temporary basis. Check out fabric samples. Paint a large poster the very color you think you cannot live without — then hang it on the wall for a week. Take furnishings home on approval to see if that is what you really want. As for placement, draw your room out on paper, and move cutouts of your furniture to different spots until you are happy with it. That way, your movers will not lose their good backs, nor your decorator his temper.

Some people say, "Why do I even need a decorator? I took a course online and now I can do it myself." The truth is that true decorators learn some of those same rules, but the difference is that good decorators learn much more. Art, intuition, and experience help us use the rules to more advantage, or to know when and where we can break a few of them to create the perfect space. We also know how to find the best products and finest original pieces for the best price.

So work with your decorator. Be outspoken about your goals and tell him or her what you don't like before it becomes a permanent part of your home. If the damage is already done, work together to find the easiest solution.

I traveled all over the country and talked to thousands of people regarding decorating. As I stated before, most of the ladies had very specific questions regarding one or two design elements in their homes. They got snagged on a problem concerning paint, fabric, furnishings, or window treatments. The best thing to do when you hit a brick wall is to ask for help from a decorator who is talented and will customize the bill to the job.

Speaking of furnishings, I am going to share a little decorating secret with you. Sofas are not good looking pieces of furniture. When you see them in a furniture show room, it is in the perspective of twenty-foot ceilings where "objects appear smaller than their actual size." Then, when the movers tote that thing into your house, you realize it is really huge. It will only look bigger and bigger. Just think about that in relation to clothing: If you decide you do not like one of your dresses, you can just hang it in the closet—but you cannot hang a sofa. It is just going to sit there sprawling, yawning at you for years.

With a half-century of decorating and designing under my Gucci belt, I must have spoken at least ten million words about my work. I have run my mouth in conversations and during hundreds of speeches, but now it is time for me to quiet down and let my book do some talking. There's one thing I do not think I can ever quit, though, and that is the act of trying to help. When I survey anything, ranging from a single room to a bonafide mansion, things spring out at me that could be improved upon, and I want to help.

My name is Randy, and I am a designer and decorator, born and bred.

Fresh flowers are standard in Randy's world.

Today, Randy lives just minutes away from Wrightsville Beach in a neighborhood of upscale condominiums, but the outdoor Sunbrella draperies signal visitors that they are about to enter a different sort of high-end patio home.

A sentimental theme runs through out the house. Below, one of Randy's favorite childhood toys, a Charlie McCarthy marionette, leans against his parents' old clock from Arlington Avenue.

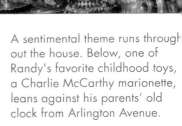

Left: Randy sleeps here, too. The memory of Mabel Trull, her image caught on canvas, stays "ever gentle" on his mind.

PRINCESS SLEEPS HERE

Acknowledgments

ANYONE WHO IS FOOLISH enough to come into my shop in Wilmington, North Carolina gets an earful from me about the merchandise and how much I love designing, what I have designed, and what crazy things I have done in my seventy-nine years. Yet, what I usually think about when I am alone is where I am going and which new ideas will work best. I don't think about history. I think about today and tomorrow. Today, I want to stir things up as much as possible. Tomorrow, I want to unveil another new idea that will serve a need in the market—and bring me many rewards.

My life today is less hectic than my years were in New York. I get up in the morning and take Princess for her walk. Then, I make coffee, something I did not drink until a few years ago. Face it: Do I really need caffeine? I read the local newspaper, paying close attention to the bridge game section, then disagree with how they played it. "Gosh," I always think. "I could have done that better!"

I head off to the office with Princess in tow. When we arrive she barks at whoever is there. All she is saying is

"Hello! Please give me a dog bone." She is utterly spoiled, but I don't care. She is in love with me and I with her. The rest of the staff just has to live with us both.

I sit down at my desk and listen, not very well, to whatever they have to tell me. This is nothing new. My mind has always wandered. Just the other day while someone was talking to me about something or another, I thought, "Gosh, why not design placemats out of Sunbrella? They would be beautiful and easy to preserve. What would be the cost? Who cares."

So even now, I am off running down a new design road. Everyone else is trying to figure out how to pay the shop overhead and worrying about the new shipment from Europe. I am not worried. I am in my dream world figuring out the details of a new idea that will drive them mad.

Pardon me for digressing again. If you have read this crazy book and wonder what the message is, don't feel alone. Maybe I should have made the "moral of the story" more plain, but here it is in simple words. Take time with your kids. Try, as my mother did, to stand beside them. Encourage and support them. Be more than just a Mom. Be their irreplaceable friend. Always keep your chin high when you view their successes, for you are the power behind the throne.

To me, this book is really about my mother, Mabel Holland Trull. She had the sensitivity to see my strengths and my weaknesses, but she always fanned the flames of my talents. She knew how to build my confidence, and she lived a life that made me proud of her, too. Drawing the card of having her as my mother was the luckiest break I ever got. My biggest portion of gratitude goes to her, but others have supported me through the process of writing, editing, and analyzing my life story:

Robert Hill Camp—the name is good and the talent is good. Little did he ever know what a madman he was working with until it was too late. He had to work hard because my writings were all over the map. He spent hours trying to make it read smoothly. I think he did a fine job in editing the tale of a wild designer who is still crazy and going strong.

Susan Taylor Block, who has written lots of books, has worked with lots of people who thought normal thoughts. Then, one day, she had the lousy break of meeting me. She agreed to help me with the book, so luck was still going for me. She has tried to keep me on the right track, teach me to spell, and bring theme and sense to my life story. What fun I have had working with her. Even though I am not thrilled to pay the money, what the heck? I do not know squat about writing a book and she has had the patience to work with me and help me finally get this book finished. Lucky me: She has been just great and now I have a friend for life.

Betty Rusher works with me in my shop three days a week, but is willing to help manage my crazy life and get me out of jams 24/7. She never says anything bad about anything or anybody. I think I almost drive her a little mad, but she doesn't even complain about me. She manages somehow to stay calm, but I imagine she thinks, "Man, this Randy is off on something else, again!" Then, I just put that "something else" in her lap and say, "Well, you know how to make this idea of mine work."

Then, with grace and a smile, Betty will make it work. What a jewel she is. I told you I was lucky. It was one of my luckiest breaks when she said she would work with me, but

I bet she was thinking, "This guy is mad. I think he lived up North too long."

Pam Millar works in my shop the balance of the week. She probably thinks I don't even like her, because I just say, "Oh, Pam, could you do this? Don't worry, Pam, it will work out somehow."

Pam tears through books and magazines like wild fire, and has read this manuscript more times than I have. She kept sticking little pink slips in it saying, "Change this. Change that." She was right, but I just don't worry about the little things. I move on to the big show. Why Pam even puts up with me I am not sure. She did go to Parsons, though, so she knew I was off the wall from day one. So, who is lucky in this friendship? Me, me, me.

Betty, Pam, and I—plus Princess—have moved mountains to make it fun and exciting to come to work at Classic Designs of Wilmington. We have become a little family that exists not only in my business world, but also in my heart. If it weren't for them, I would be even crazier.

Finally, I want to thank all y'all—for that's the Southern way, is it not?

7141089R0

Made in the USA
Charleston, SC
26 January 2011